More than money was at stake

Sudden emotion flared in Carlo's eyes as he stared at Rosanna, but a moment later it was gone, and he bowed ironically.

Rosanna smiled grimly. She felt a fraud, dressed to parade herself for a man who was a stranger…and soon to be her husband. But she had to face reality, and reality was the man standing opposite.

Carlo slipped his hand into his pocket and took out a flat box, opening it as he walked toward her. It was a necklace, the blue-and-white fire of the precious stones sparkling in the chandelier light.

"I don't care what you do with it after tonight," he said, "as long as you don't send it to the lover who's getting all the money you're earning with me."

Books by Susan Alexander

These books may be available at your local bookseller.

For a list of all titles currently available,
send your name and address to:

Harlequin Reader Service
P.O. Box 52040, Phoenix, AZ 85072-2040
Canadian address: P.O. Box 2800, Postal Station A,
5170 Yonge St., Willowdale, Ont. M2N 5T5

SUSAN ALEXANDER

the marriage contract

Harlequin Books

TORONTO • NEW YORK • LONDON
AMSTERDAM • PARIS • SYDNEY • HAMBURG
STOCKHOLM • ATHENS • TOKYO • MILAN

Harlequin Presents first edition September 1984
ISBN 0-373-10719-6

Original hardcover edition published in 1983
by Mills & Boon Limited

CHAPTER ONE

THE heat slapped against her body like a thick blanket, enveloping her completely as she stepped down on to the tarmac, the hot wind stinging her bare legs and forcing tears to her eyes. Reaching for her dark glasses, she made her way towards the airport buildings with the other half dozen first class passengers.

'Aeroporto Palermo'.

In huge letters the sign soared above the building, etched against the unclouded blue of the Sicilian sky. By the time they passed into the cool dark interior, her cotton dress was sticking to her skin. Waiting for her luggage, she wondered if she would be met. There had been no mention of it in her instructions. Should she find a porter? Get a taxi?

'Signorina Dunham?'

She turned to see an airport official in impeccable grey uniform bowing formally, his eyes questioning.

She nodded and he smiled broadly, white teeth flashing, his dark eyes on the blonde of her hair.

'Please to follow me.' He walked ahead, leading the way out of the building.

'My luggage . . .? she queried.

'Will follow in a moment,' he answered smoothly.

They emerged into airport reception to a crowd of waiting relatives and friends. Her guide continued without stopping, clearing a way for them both to the exit doors which opened automatically, and once more she was out in the white glare of the midday sun. The forecourt was lined with long sleek coaches waiting for their allotted parties of holidaymakers, brightly uniformed couriers chatting in groups.

Turning sharply, her guide headed for a large black Mercedes, its dark-tinted windows gleaming in the sun, a small blue and gold flag rampant on the bonnet. A uniformed chauffeur straightened at their approach and saluted smartly.

'*Buon giorno, signorina.*' He handed her into the rear of the limousine, taking her coat and bag to put on the front seat. The two men exchanged a quiet word, a porter emerged from the airport buildings with her cases, some money changed hands and the bags were stored in the boot. She smiled vaguely at the farewell salute from the airport official as the car slid smoothly out of the airport and on to the *autostrada* to Palermo.

Rosanna leaned back, eyes closed, as the heat receded from her face and body in the cool of the air-conditioning.

A quiet hum sounded and she opened her eyes to see the glass partition slide down between herself and the chauffeur. In the mirror above his head she could see a dark-eyed Sicilian in his forties, broadly built and darkly tanned with thick black curly hair escaping from under the peaked cap, his smile friendly and impersonal.

'My name is Enrico, *signorina*,' he explained. 'Your plane was late and we are a little behind schedule, but I will now try to make up the time. Forgive me if I do not converse. If you wish to speak to me, please use the tube at your elbow.'

He smiled again briefly and the partition rose once more, shutting her off. She looked down at the old-fashioned tube and glanced round at the luxury of thick carpet and suede leather upholstery. Sudden nausea rose in her throat and she swallowed convulsively as panic threatened. Fighting back to resist it, she determined to remain cool, refusing to allow her imagination to riot away with her common sense. Nothing could be gained if she gave way to panic. Resolutely she looked out at her surroundings.

The heat rose in shimmering waves from the tarmac of the motorway, and was reflected back from the white dusty roadway as they turned off towards Palermo. On both sides houses were shuttered and shops empty, spilling their wares on to pavements deserted during the midday heat.

As they neared the city, the atmosphere changed. Where the big silent car had sped quietly and fast through deserted suburbs, they were now surrounded on all sides by traffic, people and noise. Car windows wound down, drivers were hurling angry insults at each other while hooters blasted, brakes squealed and tiny cars, daring and defiant, whipped in and out of traffic lanes.

Darkly mellowed stone of square majestic buildings towered above modern, elegant, glass-fronted shops, cars and people reflected in their sparkling windows. Crowds thronged the pavement cafés, sitting in the shade of gaily striped umbrellas, seemingly unperturbed by the frenzy of traffic only a few feet away.

Enrico continued expertly. Crossing the large square with its ornate stone fountain, he raised his hand in casual salute to the white-helmeted policeman who waved them on from his pedestal, his piercing whistle clenched between dazzling teeth.

Two more turnings and they were in a tree-lined avenue flanked on both sides by shuttered town villas set back in brilliantly coloured gardens, soaring spiked brass railings guarding the privacy of their owners.

Enrico swung sharply into a driveway and the gates opened automatically. The big car crunched to a stop on the gravel, and Rosanna had a quick glimpse of the red and gold Orsini crest above the heavy oak front door, before Enrico ushered her out of the car and she walked into the chilly darkness of the house.

The sudden contrast with the brilliant light outside blinded her for a moment and she didn't see the woman who stood waiting. Nervously she blinked at the cavernous hall with its black ebony panelled walls, huge dark mosaic floor and wide wooden staircase sweeping to the upper stories.

'*Buon giorno, signorina.*'

Rosanna turned. The woman was elderly, dressed in black to the floor, grey hair drawn severely upwards from a smooth round face, the small eyes dark and cold.

'I am Sophia, the housekeeper,' she said, her voice expressionless. '*Il signore* is expecting you.'

She turned and led the way. Their feet made no noise up the thickly carpeted stairs, and the sombre portraits in their heavy gold frames stared woodenly as the two women climbed. High above in the domed roof hung a large gilded cage suspended from heavy coiled black cabling—a lift.

On the first floor the housekeeper continued through a maze of windowless corridors, the only sound the faint swish of her dress as it swept the tiled floor, the only light from yellow glass goblets blurred with age, supported against the wall in black wrought-iron holders.

Sophia stopped at last in front of a double wooden door and knocked. It was opened immediately and, heart hammering, Rosanna stepped across the threshold.

The room was empty. She turned to see a young man closing the door behind the housekeeper.

'*Signorina*,' he said quietly, and bowed. In spite of the intense heat of the day he was dressed in formal suit and tie, his face grave and pale, the eyes hidden behind thick, round steel-rimmed glasses. '*Un momento*,' he said. 'I will see if *il signore* can receive you now. Please take a seat.'

He disappeared through a far door and Rosanna sat down on the edge of a high backed chair in the middle of the room.

The silence was complete. No murmur of voices or sound of footfalls reached her. The shutters were closed and in the dim light she could barely see into the dark corners of the ornately furnished high-ceilinged room.

Her control was beginning to slip, and she could feel the fear crawl along her skin. The urge to run was overwhelming, and she clenched her hands hard, digging her nails into her palms as panic brought the blood rushing to her head and she began to feel faint. She wished she had eaten something on the plane. Suddenly England seemed a lifetime away as she recognised the difference between working everything out calmly and rationally a thousand miles away, and being in this house, waiting to face the man she had come to see.

'*Signorina*.' The young man was standing in the open doorway. He gestured for her to come, but suddenly she couldn't move. Fear kept her glued to her chair. She couldn't go through with it. She had to get out of the house, back to the airport and on to the next plane home. Home! There was no home . . . not any more.

She lifted her head and clenched the muscles of her

legs, forcing herself to get up and move across the room, hoping her knees wouldn't buckle as she walked slowly past him into the room beyond.

The first thing that struck her was the heat. The room was stifling, and even the midday sun couldn't account for it. In the silence the hum of a fan heater reached her. The room was heated artificially.

'Rosanna Dunham.'

It was a statement, not a question, and she swung round towards the voice.

Seated in a deep winged armchair, supported by cushions, a rug covering his legs, sat Roberto Orsini. The granite face with its halo of white hair, the strong powerful nose and the lipless wide mouth were all strange to her. But the eyes she knew as she knew her own. They were her mother's eyes. This was indeed her grandfather.

'Well?' The voice was unexpectedly steely.

She felt her tongue cleave to the roof of her mouth and knew if she tried to speak she would stammer. That legacy from her childhood always returned at times of acute stress. So she stood silent as he looked up at her, his glance travelling from the heavy swathe of her shoulder-length blonde hair to the deep almost purple-black of her eyes, down the tall, slender figure in its shabby dress to the long slim legs and cheap sandals on her feet.

'Sit down,' he commanded.

'I'd rather stand.' her voice came cool and clear. She sighed with relief, expelling her breath slowly, keeping the stammer at bay.

He leaned back. 'So you're the only child of my daughter?' he affirmed haughtily. His voice was strong, inflexible, the voice of a much younger man. Rosanna remained silent. 'Well ...' he demanded arrogantly, 'are you a Dunham or an Orsini?'

'Both,' she replied proudly. And suddenly every-thing clicked into place as memory flooded her mind, driving out nervousness and fear. The reason why she was in this room, the deep fierce hatred she felt for the man sitting opposite, apparently so weak and helpless, yet responsible with his ruthless and vindictive pride for the sufferings of her father and mother.

He must have seen the thoughts chase across her face. 'So,' he observed harshly, 'you show your hatred and contempt. Are you not afraid I'll terminate the contract before it has begun?'

'No,' she responded coldly, 'I'm not afraid. I feared you once when you had the power to hurt my parents, but now there's no one left to hurt. There's only me. And you'll never reach me with your cruelty!' Her voice rang young and clear in the darkened room, and the old man reacted to it. His lips twisted and his eyes flashed with anger.

'So,' he rasped, 'I am the villain still?'

'I have no wish to argue with you,' she said more quietly. 'I'm only here on business.'

'On whoring business,' he snarled, and she caught her breath at the contempt in his voice. 'You come here to sell yourself for money, and you dare hurl your pride into my face. Have you no shame?'

'I'm here to fulfil a simple contract,' she managed with dignity, her trembling hands behind her back, 'but that doesn't give you the right to abuse me, nor am I prepared to listen to your opinion of my morals.' Her cool was beginning to crack and she wished he would get to the end of this interview.

'Very well,' he agreed more quietly, 'as soon as you sit down, I'll go over the arrangements. You are tall and I don't propose to crane my neck to talk to you.'

Rosanna sat down on the nearest chair, the wood hard against her legs. They were now face to face, and he looked straight into her eyes as he began to talk, slowly and evenly without emotion. 'It is agreed you will provide me with an heir by the man I have chosen. On the day of your marriage you will receive ten thousand pounds sterling. On the day you give birth to the child you will receive a further twenty thousand. When the child is weaned he will be handed over to me. You will then give up any rights to him, leave Sicily and never see him again. A divorce will then be arranged.'

Rosanna said nothing. He wasn't telling her anything she didn't know. As the silence lengthened in the heated room, she looked across at her grandfather and found him staring at her intently. Her eyes widened apprehensively. Was there something more, something else she didn't know?

'Well, have you no questions, girl?' he demanded harshly. 'Aren't you curious? What if I'm marrying you to a monster, a fiend or even a pervert?'

She clenched her jaw in an effort to control the fear that racked her body at his words. He was touching on the dread of her most terrible nightmares. She swallowed heavily, clearing her throat, fighting for coherent thought, determined he shouldn't see her fear.

'Since you want an heir of your own blood you aren't likely to pick a maniac for his father,' she managed at last.

'Mighty cool,' he sneered.

Rosanna spoke quickly. 'What if the baby is a girl? What will happen to her? Will you ignore her, tyrannise her as you did my mother, so that she too will do anything to get away from her unhappy life?'

She saw the terrible anger in his face before he spoke. 'You are insolent!' He was breathing with difficulty. 'And about things you don't understand. If the child is a girl she will be my heir and brought up to it . . . just as your mother was.' The raw anger changed to a grunt as he bent across his clenched hands, doubled up with pain. Reaching for a small bottle from the table at his side, he opened it and swallowed some of the pills. Rosanna watched, impassive, as the colour returned slowly to the ashen skin. Only a slight tremor of her mouth revealed a moment's compassion as she watched his desperate fight for breath. She was determined there would be no emotion between them, and there was no pity in her eyes as she waited.

At last he sat up, his head resting against the high back of the chair, hands gripping his knees through the heavy blanket.

'Tomorrow morning at eleven o'clock you will meet here in this house with Don Carlo and the contract will be signed.' He paused, his breathing still painful, and Rosanna felt an overwhelming urge to leave . . . to get away from the suffocation of the room. She got up.

'Very well, I'll be here. I'll leave now and find myself a hotel.'

'No!' he thundered at her. 'How dare you suggest that an Orsini bride will go to her wedding from a hotel? You'll remain in this house until you remove from it to the house of your husband. A suite of rooms has been prepared.' His voice sank with exhaustion. 'After tomorrow there will be no need for us to . . . meet again.'

She turned to leave.

'Your mother . . .' his voice stopped her. 'She is dead?'

Rosanna quivered with feeling. This was the test. She must not give herself away. Slowly she turned back to him. 'Yes,' she said baldly.

'Where is she buried?' he asked quietly.

'It is not part of my contract to furnish you with information,' she replied coldly.

He sighed. 'You are not like your mother.'

'No,' she said clearly, 'fortunately for us both.'

For a moment they stared at each other, exchanging looks almost of recognition, as of enemies sizing up their opponents. Rosanna thought she saw a fleeting look of some emotion in his eyes. Was it admiration? And then it was gone and she knew herself to have been mistaken.

Suddenly the door opened behind her and a plump, middle-aged nurse in white starch hurried past her to the old man.

'That's quite enough damage for one day,' she said severely in Italian. 'Back to bed immediately. Please go now, *signorina*,' she added coldly and dismissively over her shoulder.

Rosanna woke to a darkened room wondering for a moment where she was. Then memory returned. Sophia had led her from her grandfather's suite to the floor above where she found a sitting room, bedroom and bathroom had been put at her disposal. Her clothes had been unpacked and looked particularly insignificant in the vast mahogany wardrobe. Heedless of the heavy luxury of her surroundings or the cold lunch set out for her, she had lain down on the bed to fall immediately asleep. She stretched pleasurably, her head clear, the ache of tiredness gone from her eyes. In her robe she padded across to the shutters and opened them wide, to find herself at the back of the house. Down below the garden was surrounded by a tight high fringe of dark cypresses that cast their shadows over the brilliant blue of the swimming pool. The heat was muted and the shadows lengthening, and Rosanna felt a sudden urge to walk to lose herself among people, away from the heavy oppressiveness of the house.

Ten minutes later she let herself out, the movement of the heavy bolt on the massive front door the only sound in the silent villa.

Back in the main thoroughfare she had crossed earlier in the day the atmosphere was very different. Shops were open and doing brisk business. Pavements were crowded with people moving at leisure and enjoying the balm of early evening. There was still traffic, but moving slowly, the chatter of drivers friendly and cheerful as they waited for the jams to ease. The fountain in the centre of the square was alive with children, their excited cries to each other punctuated intermittently by the shrill warnings from their watching mammas.

Unconscious of admiring glances from several pairs of dark eyes on the shimmering blonde of her hair, Rosanna wandered, a curious contentment relaxing her mind and slowing her steps. She breathed in the cooling air, her attention held by the dazzling displays in the shop windows she passed.

There were soft elegant leather goods in shades of deepest burgundy to palest greys; flowers exquisitely arranged behind plate glass windows awash with sprays of water keeping the atmosphere fresh and moist; and lacy underwear in silks, satins and chiffons, from carnation pink to mint greens and the deepest black of frothy nightgowns widely edged with lace.

Engrossed in what she saw, it was a moment before

Rosanna became aware of a face close to hers. Turning her head, she watched a young man in the act of cutting the straps of her handbag. Before she had fully grasped what he was doing, he had severed the bag from the strap and, with a quick impudent smile, melted away into the crowd, leaving Rosanna with the strap still firmly clutched in her hand.

'Oh, no . . .!' her cry was involuntary. The bag contained everything—her money, passport, papers. . . . 'Stop, thief!' she called loudly in Italian, and several people turned to look. The thief, too, halted a moment, surprised at her knowledge of Italian. 'Please . . . stop him!' she begged as he began to run and she struggled along the crowded pavement in his wake.

Someone tried to halt him and caught his arm. A woman shouted and a clamour of voices erupted as Rosanna stepped off the pavement and began to run.

Suddenly there was a high-pitched scream, a screech of brakes, and she felt something hard pushing into the middle of her back. She turned, reaching out blindly to catch at anything to break her fall, but there was nothing there. Plunging forward across the bonnet of a car, she slid senseless to the ground.

Rosanna opened her eyes to find herself lying in the road. Faces loomed above, all looking down at her, a babel of voices raised in argument. Weakly she tried to get up, but a hard hand pushed her back.

'Please, *signorina*, do not move,' a forceful masculine voice reached her as her head began to swim, and she lay back. 'Now,' the same voice continued, 'stand back, please. . . .' The voices receded slightly and Rosanna tried to open her eyes, but the lids felt oddly leaden and wouldn't move.

Then she felt hands on her, capable, impersonal,

feeling her all over, probing her neck, across her shoulders and down her legs. 'I am Dottore Albini, *signorina*,' a quiet voice said. 'In a moment we will move you. Please keep quite still.'

She was lifted in strong arms, her head pressed against a silk shirt through which she could feel a hard masculine chest and smell a faintly astringent cologne. She ached all over and was relieved when the arms put her down on to soft cushions and covered her with a rug as she began to tremble with cold.

She must have slept, because the next thing she felt was being lifted again.

'I can walk,' she said crossly in English. And then she fainted.

The next time she opened her eyes it was to an unfamiliar room and the murmur of masculine voices. Carefully she raised her head and pain shot across her shoulders and down her arms. Weakly she lay back, allowing her gaze to wander round the room.

She was lying on a couch covered with a duvet. Opposite was a large picture window running the length of one wall, and beyond it she could make out stone balcony railings and the Palermo skyline. Inside she glimpsed whitewashed walls, terracotta tiles on the floor and light modern furniture. At her side a large round glass-topped coffee table and several deep tubular-framed leather chairs were grouped round a brick fireplace, its brass fittings gleaming in the light from several ceiling spot lamps casting a soft glow over the room. Against one wall was a pale pine unit with stereo equipment and above it hung two rather arresting wild seascapes mounted and unframed in the modern idiom.

Moving more slowly, she tried again to sit up. The

voices stopped and a man came towards her.

'That's better,' he said in careful English. Putting a hand against her forehead, he laid her gently back on to the cushions. 'I'm Doctor Albini,' he went on in English, drawing up a stool to sit at her side. 'I've brought you here because the roads to the hospital are jammed with traffic. I believe there's nothing broken, but I want to examine you properly tomorrow at the hospital.' He looked down into her face. 'Do you understand what I'm saying?'

She nodded and he reached for her wrist to take a pulse reading. He was around fifty with a long, clever, rather serious face, a heavy dark jowl, black eyes and a receding hairline. His fingers were cool on her skin.

'When you get home,' he went on easily, 'I wish you to go directly to bed. You are in shock and the best thing is sleep. I have to leave you now. A drink is being prepared and then you'll be driven to your hotel.'

He stood up and waited irresolutely as though there was something else he wished to say, his warm eyes strangely concerned. Then he seemed to come to a decision. 'Questions can wait until tomorrow. *Arrivederci.*' He turned and left.

Rosanna closed her eyes. Oh, dear, she thought, why did this have to happen? Would her grandfather hear of it? Would there be trouble? Had anyone else been hurt?

'Drink this,' a quiet masculine voice commanded, and she opened her eyes to see a hand place a cup on the table beside her. The sweet liquid cleared her head and dispersed the giddiness.

'Thank you.' She placed the cup carefully back on to the table. Looking up, she saw the man pouring himself a drink, his back to her at the other side of the room. Unusually tall for a Sicilian, he was broad-shouldered but of slender build, with slim hips and long straight legs, his cream linen suit formally styled.

Suddenly he turned, and a shock flashed through Rosanna at the unexpected savagery of his face. Thick black hair, heavily streaked with grey, swept back from a widely boned forehead. Straight black brows jutted thickly above deep set eyes, their intense hard blue just visible below heavy lids, the colour vivid against the darkly tanned skin. A slender, almost patrician nose gave an aristocratic air to the head, in contrast to the powerful jaw and deeply clefted chin below a wide mouth so tightly compressed it denied any natural shape to the lips.

Rosanna stared in fascination. She had never seen a face like it. In its way handsome and compelling, but all masculine strength and arrogance, with no hint of kindness or compassion.

Suddenly she was conscious of his gaze on her face as his eyes travelled across the wide forehead, the tracery of blonde eyebrows over black-lashed dark eyes, pale, creamy skin, high cheekbones and a slender nose. His eyes lingered for a moment on her mouth, the soft outline of firmly moulded lips, and the round determined chin below.

'Well?' he drawled. 'Do you think you'd recognise me again?'

Rosanna blushed furiously as he laughed softly, but she noticed his smile was mechanical, leaving the eyes hard with boredom. She looked away. Who was he? Had he been the driver of the car that ran her down? Or merely a passer-by? His next words enlightened her.

'Like a child,' he said grimly, his smile dying, 'just wandering into the road, heedless of everything but its own immediate concern. Had I not been slowing for a corner you would be dead and I a murderer.' The voice was quiet and low-pitched, so that for a moment Rosanna didn't take in what he had said.

'I'm sorry,' she began hesitantly, 'I do realise . . . no blame attaches to you. I ran into the road to stop a thief.'

He didn't respond, and an uneasy silence settled between them. Painfully she pushed herself forward on the deep sofa and bent to retrieve her sandals. After a moment she cast aside the duvet and rose unsteadily to her feet.

'May I ask you to order me a taxi?' She leaned heavily against the arm of the sofa. Ignoring her request, he turned away to stand at the window facing out on to the darkening skyline. Still he said nothing, and she wondered if she should just go.

'If you'll let me know how much I owe you for . . . your trouble and any damage to . . . your car. . . .' she began.

'Money,' he interrupted, his voice still soft, barely raised above a murmur, but Rosanna sensed an undertone of anger that vibrated in the silent room. 'Is that all you tourists ever think about? You come to our island in your thousands, to admire its beauties and treasures. But once you're here you ignore our traditions, trample on our customs, and your only obsession is what your precious money can buy more cheaply here than in your own country. And if that money is threatened, you become hysterical, causing accidents to life and limb.'

There was a stunned silence and Rosanna began to tremble with weakness. She ignored what he had said and tried again. 'I can only repeat, *signore*, I'm sorry. And now I must go. . . .'

She moved towards the door, but his voice stopped her. 'Tell me,' he asked softly, 'why do you choose our island? What do you hope to find here that the tourist resorts of other countries don't supply?'

Rosanna wondered at his anger. She had apologised. It had been an accident and she had offered him damages. What more could she do?'

'Perhaps it is the stories that your countrywomen carry back to their homes,' his voice was silky now, 'of our young men who wait at the airports for unaccompanied women looking for adventure that is not included in their package tours?'

She froze as she realised what he was saying in that deceptively quiet voice.

'Little do they realise,' he drawled, the bored indifference back in his tone, 'our men have no respect for such women and use them in a way not permitted by our own girls, who are taught from an early age to guard their virtue as a gift to the man who weds them.'

Rosanna forgot her weakness in a sudden spurt of anger. 'You have no right to talk in this way of my countrywomen!' she snapped, her voice chilled with pride. 'I could as easily criticise Sicilian men for keeping their women in bondage a hundred years out of date. Where women have no choice, all men are masters.' She turned away and opened the door. 'Please excuse me now. I'll find my own way out.'

'Just a moment. . . .'

'No, *signore*, you mistake. I will not stay to be insulted!'

He turned to face her and she looked across the room at him, head up, eyes defiant, tears of weakness glistening on her lashes.

'Forgive me.' His smile was sudden and devastating, white teeth flashing, mobile lips revealed in sudden contrition. 'I'm guilty of bad manners. Please . . . I have no wish to insult. Much rather, I would you permit me, *signorina*, to make amends for your injury today.'

The abrupt change of manner was so surprising, Rosanna looked at him in total astonishment, wondering for one ghastly moment if he was going to offer her money. She opened her mouth to refuse, stepping back involuntarily as he moved towards her. It was then she saw the deadly boredom in those blue eyes. Before she could reply he spoke again.

'Will you allow me to show you something of Palermo during your stay something that is perhaps not on your tourist programme?' he asked silkily.

She saw in his face the arrogant assurance that she would accept his very doubtful invitation. No thought crossed his mind that she might refuse. She had never met anyone with such colossal conceit and was tempted to laugh in his face. But he was by now too near for comfort and waiting for her reply.

'Thank you,' she said indifferently, 'but as you pointed out, it is the young men at the airports who supply the services you offer. There's no need to burden yourelf with my needs.'

In the stunned silence that followed her words, he halted in his stride, only the tightly clenched jaw revealing the fury she had aroused. The hush lengthened, and she guessed he wouldn't speak until he had complete control over his anger.

'Your face has innocence, *signorina*,' he said at last, 'and your hands are ringless, but the authority in your voice reveals experience of men.' He had recovered and the smooth voice purred. 'I must suppose I'm to be denied your company because an escort—a friend awaits you.'

'You may suppose what you wish, *signore*,' she snapped. 'My private life is not open for discussion with strangers.'

'Emancipation is rife in your country, *signorina*,' he commented coldly, 'and I'm well acquainted with those of your sex who enjoy it. But you will permit me to suggest your women lose a great deal of feminine dignity and charm in their deadly pursuit of equality with men.'

'How dare you!' Rosanna was roused to fury and lashed out. 'We may not be in purdah, but we are respected by our men and taught from an early age to recognise those of your sex who wish to take advantage of our freedom to degrade us for their amusement. From their insults we learn to protect ourselves.'

His smile was mocking, devoid of all amusement. 'So you can protect yourself?' he asked softly with a small laugh. 'You speak like a child. No woman can protect herself from a man determined to take her. That is something too easily forgotten by your liberated sex.'

In two strides he was at her side, his hands gripping her shoulders, his fingers biting into the soft skin of her bare arms. She felt the steel of his embrace a moment before he bent his head to her mouth and her breath caught in her throat at the brutal onslaught of that kiss. Without desire, seeking only to punish, he forced her lips apart and ravaged her mouth to assuage his anger and wounded pride.

Faintness hit her and she went limp in his arms, desperate for air. At last he lifted his head and she gulped deeply, fighting to collect her senses. Looking up into his face, she saw a flash of surprise in those blue eyes before they were veiled with heavy lids.

For a moment they were both motionless and her

eyes widened as she saw the grim mouth relaxed, revealing firmly moulded lips, full and sensual. Then his arms fell away from her and she was free.

'My chauffeur will drive you home,' he said tonelessly, and strode from the room.

CHAPTER TWO

ROSANNA leaned forward to peer more closely into the mirror. No, she thought, the bruise didn't show. She had dressed her hair carefully to fall across the livid purple mark where she must have hit the bonnet of the car.

Her thoughts returned to the previous evening. Left alone by her host, she had panicked. In spite of weakness and pain she had stumbled out of the house, frightened that she might be followed. With no money to pay for a taxi, the return journey had been a nightmare, and it was nearly an hour before she found herself back at the Villa Orsini, relieved that the footman who let her in hadn't seen her before.

Unobserved, she had slipped to her own rooms and locked herself in to collapse on the bed. During the night she had woken to the aches and pains of her bruised body and immersed herself in a hot bath, then, falling back into bed, she had slept dreamlessly till woken by the maid with her breakfast.

And now downstairs waited the final act of the drama she had started so many months before. And from somewhere she would have to find the courage to take the last irrevocable step.

She knew, whatever it cost, she would go through with it. Here in Sicily, a thousand miles away from her mother, Rosanna could feel her presence. This house was, after all, her mother's childhood home on the island she adored. Long ago Rosanna's commitment to her mother had been made. As a child she had sensed her mother's loneliness in the country of her adoption, and had listened eagerly to stories of Sicily, its warmth, its beauty and its heritage—stories her mother never tired of repeating. As Rosanna had learned from infancy to speak Italian, so she came to know all about the pampered wealth and seclusion in which her mother had been reared—an heiress to a vast fortune, an arranged marriage before her and a widowed father her only companion.

Her mother had been just eighteen when she had met Captain Dunham, resplendent in his officer's uniform, and had fallen irrevocably in love. Silvana Orsini was the most beautiful thing Harry Dunham had ever seen—small, exquisite, with a pale oval face, the melting dark Orsini eyes and gleaming midnight black hair. With his tall blond, slim good looks they made a stunning couple, and for months Silvana had tried to persuade her father at least to meet the young English officer. But in the end the young couple became desperate, with the date of Silvana's arranged marriage approaching. And so Silvana had eloped from her father's house one dark winter afternoon, taking nothing and destined never to return.

At first things had gone well. They were in love, and two years later when Rosanna had been born, she knew her parents had both adored her. But then her father had become restless. Forced to leave his family behind when he was posted, he was lonely and decided to leave the Army, try civilian life.

Sadly things hadn't turned out as he'd hoped. He missed the social life with his brother officers the security and privileges the Army offered. And he couldn't seem to find his feet in civilian jobs. They moved into the country, renting a small cottage on an isolated farm, and her father was rarely in work. He began to feel more and more guilty that he couldn't provide for his family, while her mother was convinced she was the cause of his changed circumstances.

Rosanna never knew when her father began to drink, because her mother kept it from her in the early years. All she knew was that he was often ill and money was scarce, although her mother never complained. As Rosanna grew into a leggy teenager she learnt what her father's illness really was. And then her nightmares began. When he had been drinking he often became violent and couldn't control his rages—at fate, at the Army and at Silvana's father who steadfastly refused to help them.

Her mother had written to Roberto Orsini, asking for forgiveness and begging for help to have her husband cured. A letter came back from the Orsini family solicitors setting out the terms for her grandfather's help. Harry Dunham would have to enter a clinic and Silvana would have to agree to return to Sicily with her daughter, promising never to return to England or see her husband again.

Until the day that letter arrived Rosanna had never seen her mother angry. The letter was burnt and her mother never mentioned it again. But her father continued to vent his anger against his father-in-law, and Rosanna grew up convinced Roberto Orsini could have saved her father's health. For months Rosanna's mother was too proud to go for help, but in the end a doctor had to be called.

He told her mother bluntly that Harry Dunham's liver was almost totally destroyed, and that he could only survive if he gave up alcohol completely and at once. Failing that, there could be only one end to the illness.

Rosanna was eighteen when her father died, and she felt only a numbed relief, hardly able to remember the love and laughter of the father she had adored in early childhood. But for her mother it was quite different. She mourned her husband as though all his life he had remained the young, ardent Army officer she had loved and married. The bad years the recent terrible times seemed to recede from her mother's memory as though they had never happened.

Rosanna had left school thankfully at sixteen and begun work as a junior in the village library, where she did well, although she earned little. She hoped the worrying years were behind them and determined to care for her mother. But her mother's grief continued unabated and she sank more and more deeply into depression, eating little, sleeping badly, with no interest in anything, and each morning it became harder for Rosanna to leave her. She rushed home at lunchtime and again as soon as she finished work at night, often dreading what she might find.

Eventually Rosanna determined something had to be done. Armed with a letter from her doctor, she had travelled to London's Harley Street, where the specialist explained patiently that he would have to see her mother, and suggested a short stay in his clinic for tests and observation.

Rosanna rifled through her mother's jewellery and found her engagement ring, bought when Harry Dunham was careless of the future and deeply in love. She sold it and persuaded her reluctant mother to go for three days to Mr Martin's clinic, set in acres of beautiful grounds in the heart of Surrey. After some protestations her mother settled into the quiet luxury of good food, expert nursing care and Rosanna's daily visits. Even after three days Rosanna could see the improvement in her mother's spirits.

Mr Martin's diagnosis was adamant. Only slow regular therapy, a strict diet and constant nursing care would restore her mother's health.

They returned home and Rosanna waited to hear from the clinic about costs. When the heavy white envelope dropped through the letterbox she couldn't believe the terrible sum involved. Mr Martin was reassuring. Certainly he could treat her mother at a national hospital. It would mean a wait—six months, possibly a year, until a bed was free. Rosanna sensed her mother didn't have six months and she went to her boss. He told her there was no way he could guarantee such a loan. Why, he commented wittily, it was more than his own mortgage—and Rosanna knew then what she had to do.

The next evening after she settled her mother till she was dozing quietly, she sat down at the kitchen table and wrote to her grandfather.

Recalling only too vividly what had happened the last time he was asked for help, she determined not to make the same mistake. And so the fabrication began.

She wrote that her mother had died, that she, Rosanna, had been left penniless and had received no education. She needed urgently to borrow a large sum of money. She was young and healthy and would repay it in time, even if it took the rest of her life. She would agree to any plan for payments.

The answer came two weeks later, and was clear and explicit. No mention was made in the letter of regret at the death of her mother—his only child. There was just a detailed list of commands setting out the terms of the loan. Disgusted, Rosanna had thrown it aside, dismissing it as the whim of an ageing madman.

But her mother's condition continued to deteriorate.

She seemed to be losing all touch with reality, living in a fantasy world where Rosanna couldn't reach her. And Rosanna began to fear that hopes of recovery were being impaired.

She pulled out the letter. A year out of her life in exchange for her mother's health. A year of intimacy with a stranger that would be totally distasteful, an invasion of her deepest privacy. Could she do it?

For several nights she wrestled with the problem. She had never had any friendships with men—indeed she had never wanted any. The feelings described by her school friends and later her workmates were alien to her, and she had always assumed she wasn't normal. So she would be facing something she knew nothing about: a relationship with a man and bearing his child. Women did endure both experiences without apparent damage.

All the time she thought about it she knew what her answer would be. A week later she sent her reply and booked her mother into Mr Martin's clinic.

After that events took her over. Letters came and went, official documents, health certificates, travel documents. Somewhere an efficient machine had been set in motion.

Her parting from her mother Rosanna kept deliberately cheerful. She had explained carefully that a job abroad had come up and would pay enough for the clinic. When she got back they would find a new home, make a fresh start. Her mother was anxious, worried at her being away, but Rosanna had managed to reassure her and travelled to London with a heavy heart.

Strangely, the most difficult moments had been with Mr Williams. Harold Williams was the family solicitor, and she had gone to him with various documents that needed signatures. He was the only person to know where she was really going.

Watching him go through the familiar ritual of polishing his glasses, she wondered uneasily if she should have gone to a stranger, someone who didn't know her at all.

Adjusting his glasses, he looked at her over the top. 'Are you sure,' he asked sadly, 'this is the only way, the right thing to do?' He paused, embarrassed, trying to find the right words. 'I've known you since you were a tiny child, Rosanna, and we both know your mother would never have permitted anything like this if she'd been asked.'

'Yes,' Rosanna answered flatly, 'I know.'

'Yes ... well ...' he was a little startled at her bluntness, 'I ... it's all very noble, of course, my dear, but perhaps you don't quite realise. ...' He hesitated again awkwardly. 'I mean, you're young and ... er ... innocent, and you don't really ... know what it all means.' He stopped fussing with pens and paper for a moment and looked at her intently for a moment. 'I don't like it, Rosanna,' he said rather forcefully. 'I don't like it one little bit.'

'Would you rather I went to someone else?' Rosanna asked quietly.

He drew himself up. 'Certainly not! If anyone's to handle it for you, it will be me.'

He accepted it as Rosanna knew he would. She sold their furniture and belongings and left his fee with a reluctant Mr Williams. Then she bought herself an open return ticket from Palermo. Just in case, she thought.

Rosanna got to her feet. It was time to go downstairs.

She looked at herself in the mirror. She was wearing her only good summer dress a pale lime linen sheath with a simple round neck edged with piping. Her face looked back at her, shadowed and scared. Pulling her shoulders back and lifting her head, she gave a last tweak at the hair lying across her forehead, then, trying to still the nervous trembling of her hands, she left the room.

The house was hushed and oppressive as on the previous day. She walked slowly down the stairs and along the corridors to her grandfather's suite. The large double door was open, and the same young man rose from behind a desk as she appeared. She could hear the murmur of voices from the next room, and this time there was no wait. She was ushered immediately into her grandfather's room.

She was prepared for the intense heat, but stopped short on the threshold as the hum of conversation died at her appearance and she saw a sea of masculine faces turned towards her.

'Ah, Rosanna!' Her grandfather broke the silence and she turned to him, greeting him with a tight little smile that didn't reach her eyes 'Let me introduce you,' he went on smoothly. As the day before, he was seated amidst cushions and covered with a blanket, and she speculated fleetingly on his illness dismissing it from her mind the next moment as of no concern to her.

The atmosphere relaxed slightly as the men began to shuffle papers and place chairs round the room facing her grandfather. The shutters were partly open, throwing strips of brilliant sunlight and dark shadows into the room.

'Your solicitor, Signor Carelli.' Her grandfather's voice continued.

'*Signorina.*' Her hand was taken in a small soft one and she looked down at a short, rotund, balding man who looked up at her with some curiosity, his light eyes sharp in a rather colourless face. She flushed slightly and nodded without speaking. He released her hand and returned to the large desk drawn into the centre of the room and strewn with papers and documents.

'Signor Ruggieri,' her grandfather said, 'Don Carlo's solicitor.' The tall angular, raven-haired man bowed distantly and her grandfather's voice went on. 'Carlo, my granddaughter, Rosanna Dunham. Rosanna, Don Carlo Vicenzi.'

Rosanna turned as another man stepped out of the shadows and she looked into the face of her future husband.

Her gaze faltered and the room began to swim as she stared at the man who had run her down in the streets of Palermo the previous evening. She tried to focus on what he was saying, but the voice drummed in her ears and she reached desperately for the nearest chair.

Seeing her white face and swimming eyes, Don Carlo advanced towards her. Taking her shoulders between his hands he pushed her firmly down into a chair. Her head fell forward as she tried to contain the shock and control the panic that was engulfing her, but no thoughts came to help.

'Drink this.' She heard his voice, commanding as it had done the day before. She shook her head.

'Water, please,' she whispered, and heard his faint exclamation of impatience.

He returned and held the glass to her lips. It was cold and she swallowed avidly as the world began to right itself around her. 'Thank you,' she said quietly, 'it was the heat.'

'Of course,' he answered coldly, and turned away.

'Are you all right, Rosanna?' It was her grandfather, and almost she detected a note of anxiety.

'*Si, grazie.*' She turned her face towards him, a small smile embracing them all in quick apology.

'Very well.' Her grandfather began again. 'The papers are all here, ready for final signatures. After that the terms of the contract begin to operate,' he finished significantly, and she knew he was referring to the money.

As voices continued round her Rosanna tried to take in what had happened. She hadn't really given much thought to the man she would marry. Dimly in the back of her mind had been a picture of someone poor like herself, doing it for money, a man possibly old, unattractive. Never in her wildest, most desperate nightmares had she envisaged someone like Carlo Vicenzi.

Her brain drummed its question. Why? Why should he do something like this? He was obviously rich, a powerful personality with considerable attractions for women who liked dominating, ruthless men. Surely he could marry anyone he wished? So why was he lending himself to this charade? Was there some sinister reason? Once more she wondered if there was more to all this than she had been told. Her mind wound its tortuous trail in circles getting nowhere. Suddenly she heard her name.

'Rosanna, did you hear me?' her grandfather was asking.

'No, I'm sorry, I didn't.'

'Carlo is suggesting we might postpone this session until tomorrow.'

'Yes . . . oh, yes' she murmured thankfully. 'Please . . . that would be . . . I would prefer. . . .'

'Very well,' Don Carlo cut short her protestations. 'Roberto.' To Rosanna's surprise he bent to the old man and kissed him on both cheeks. Then he straightened and turned to her. 'We'll go,' he said curtly, not looking into her face.

She got up and glanced at her grandfather, meeting an intent look from his dark eyes, an expression almost of anxiety. But then it was gone, and with a quick nod to everyone Rosanna walked unsteadily through the door which Don Carlo held open for her.

Side by side they made their way silently through the outer room, oblivious of the secretary who half rose as they appeared. Once in the cool of the dim hall Rosanna drew a deep breath, filling her lungs with the air she had craved in the overheated room behind her.

Don Carlo gripped her arm and led her downstairs and out into the sunshine. She wondered where he was taking her, but had not the strength to protest or ask questions. He unlocked the silver sports car standing in the gravelled driveway, and within moments they were on their way.

The confined space of the powerful car brought sharp awareness of the man at her side. Rosanna was uncomfortably conscious of broad shoulders, long legs in tobacco brown silk, the tang of his cologne, and the masculine hands with their unexpectedly sensitive fingers resting lightly on the wheel. The bright sunlight showed him to be older than he had appeared the day before. Lines of tension were deeply etched round the mouth and she could see tiny flecks of white in the thick black brows above the deep-set eyes.

She turned away to look rather blindly out of the window. She felt no panic or revulsion. Her feelings were numb—frozen, her only certainty that she couldn't marry this man. Not for a year, not even for a single day could she be his wife, bear his child. She would have to explain to her grandfather, beg him to change the terms, find someone else. Vaguely she wondered if the man at her side would help her. He must feel the same—the mutual antagonism had been there between them from the first moment. Her grandfather appeared to be fond of Don Carlo. Perhaps they could approach him jointly.

A sudden thought intruded. Had Don Carlo known yesterday who she was? She turned her head towards him.

'No,' came the cold quiet voice, 'I didn't know who you were yesterday.' She looked at him in astonishment. 'But I did know today. The police caught the thief and your handbag was returned to me this morning. It's behind you. I saw then from your papers that I'd nearly killed my prospective bride.' His mouth curled sardonically, and she blushed.

Reaching to the back seat, she picked up her bag and clutched it in her lap as he swung the car into the entrance of a large modern building.

'Where are we going?' she asked nervously.

'The hospital.' He opened his door and got out. 'Come.'

'No,' she looked pleadingly up into his face, 'I . . . it's not necessary. I'm fine. Please . . . I'd rather not. . . .'

'You can't have looked into the mirror this morning,' he interrupted indifferently. 'Your bruise is purple and your face still in shock.'

Rosanna clenched her hands tightly over her bag and looked down, letting her hair fall forward to hide her face. Tears threatened behind her lashes. Don Carlo came round the car and opened her door, but she didn't move.

'I should tell you,' he said coldly, 'tears don't affect me. Nor do I have any patience with female tantrums. If you don't wish to walk, I'll carry you. It makes no difference.'

He moved threateningly towards her, bending as if to pick her up. She evaded him and was out of the car, brushing past him and walking ahead. Inside he took her firmly by the elbow. Without glancing right or left he walked purposefully up the stairs and along several corridors before stopping and knocking at a door marked simply G. Albini.

The nurse rose from behind her desk and showed them in at once, the two men greeting each other affectionately.

'Giorgio, *comè sta.* . . .'

'*Bene, grazie, Carlo*. . . . Ah, good morning, Miss Dunham.' The doctor gestured to a chair and turned to Don Carlo. 'Thank you, Carlo, I don't believe we'll need you now. Let me see . . . about an hour and a half, I think.'

'I'll send the car to pick you up.' Don Carlo bowed coldly to Rosanna and left.

CHAPTER THREE

THE door closed behind Don Carlo and the doctor crossed to his desk and sat down.

'Now tell me, how do you feel this morning? Headache?'

She shook her head. 'No, it's gone.'

'Good. I'm going to have some tests run first—just routine—and then you'll come back here and we'll have a little chat.' He paused and looked rather intently into her face for a moment. 'Mm,' he murmured, and pressed a button on his intercom. 'Will you please fetch Miss Dunham now?'

The next hour passed quickly. Dressed in a hospital overall, Rosanna was handed from one white-coated expert to the next while every function in her body was tested and scrutinised. Eventually she was back with Dr Albini.

'Will you please lie down on that table?' He indicated a curtained alcove, and proceeded to give her a thorough examination. He was gentle and firm, but didn't speak. At last it was over. 'Please get dressed,' he instructed. 'I'm going to have some coffee. Would that suit you, or would you prefer tea?'

'Coffee,' she answered shyly. And then she was dressed, sitting opposite him, slightly tense as he wrote up his notes. The nurse brought coffee and left them.

The doctor picked up his cup. 'Now,' he began easily, 'I haven't had all the results yet, but there appear to be no lasting ill effects from yesterday, nothing broken or torn.' Rosanna looked up at him in some relief. 'But there is something else, and perhaps you know what I'm going to say?' He looked across at her rather searchingly, noting the apprehension in her eyes.

'I h-h-had a m-m-medical examination b-b-before I l-l-left England,' she stammered, blushing deeply at the evidence of her speech impediment.

His eyes didn't waver from her face and didn't change expression. 'Did your doctor tell you you're suffering from malnutrition?' he asked bluntly.

'No.' She looked at him in astonishment. 'Why, am I?'

He nodded. 'I have to ask you some personal questions now and I'd like you to answer them quite honestly. Will you do that? It is important.'

'Yes,' she whispered.

'Do you ever feel nauseous at the sight of food?'

'Yes.'

'Often?' he rapped out.

'Yes,' she admitted.

'M . . .' he looked down at his notes. 'Do you ever go a day or longer without a meal?'

'I . . . er . . . well, if I. . . .'

'The truth,' he commanded.

'Yes,' she said quietly.

'When did this start?'

'I can't remember.'

'Try.'

'When my mother became ill I. . . .' She stopped. 'My mother,' she began again, 'was ill for a long time and I. . . .'

'I think I should tell you,' he interrupted gently, 'that Carlo has told me of your impending marriage and its rather strange circumstances.' His voice continued in the same even, impersonal tone. 'This only concerns me as far as it affects your health.'

'I see.' Rosanna was not used to talking about herself to strangers and was finding it difficult. 'My mother and I lived alone,' she went on nervously, 'and when she became ill I ... nursed her. Perhaps ... I might have got out of the habit of making meals for myself then.' She didn't tell him that all the money had gone to tempt her mother's slender appetite with delicacies, and, once the bills were paid from her own meagre salary, she often had trouble finding her bus fares to work.

'Mm. . . .' he commented again. 'Will you tell me something about your mother? I understand she was Sicilian?'

Rosanna swallowed hard. She had no wish to spin a web of lies to this man. 'Is that really necessary?' she asked hesitantly.

'I have no wish to bring up painful memories,' he said quietly, 'if you'd rather not talk about it.'

'Thank you,' she murmured weakly.

'But you must understand if you continue as you are and have a child, there could be difficulties. You're young and the child will take from you what it needs, but leave you weak, possibly ill afterwards.'

The colour rushed into her face and neck, embarrassment at his words quite evident for him to see.

'I'm a doctor,' he explained, 'and nothing said here will go any further, not even to my good friend Carlo Vicenzi. I can only guess how long this has been going on, and I respect your wishes to remain reticent. But you're making it more difficult for me to help you.' He sighed, pausing for a moment as though to find the right words. 'Have you heard of anorexia nervosa?' he asked.

'I . . . er . . . think so. But I'm not sure I know what it is.'

'It's an illness where the patient cannot eat normally. The body apparently doesn't want food, and the symptoms are usually loss of appetite, sickness after meals and lack of interest in food. Sudden desperate hunger may force the patient to eat enormous meals at infrequent intervals, and the stomach will reject such assaults. Do you follow that?'

'Yes,' she whispered, her eyes riveted to his face. He was describing exactly what happened to her frequently.

'The cause of the illness is usually nervous worry of some kind. It can be desire in adolescence for a thin figure when the body is growing and cannot be forced into a slim silhouette. It can be lack of money which is being spent on other things. The stomach shrinks and is then unable to accept normal amounts of food as the body needs it.' He smiled at her. 'I don't believe you wish to abuse your health. But loneliness or concern for a loved person has led you into habits that aren't too easy to break.'

Rosanna didn't speak and he continued, 'I've arranged with Carlo that I'll treat you for the moment. If, later, when you're married, pregnant, you wish to have an English doctor this can be arranged. But for the time being you are a stranger in Sicily, and it is agreed you'll have treatment with me.'

'Have you . . . does Don Carlo know I have this . . .?' Rosanna hesitated, biting her lip.

'Yes. I told him yesterday what I suspected—that was before we knew who you were. When he phoned me this morning and explained, he mentioned it again. Naturally he's concerned.'

Rosanna swallowed nervously. 'Now,' he went on lightly, 'the treatment is very simple. I want you to stop worrying about food. Any meal you have will be accompanied by a dish of what I call nibbles—pieces of cheese, nuts, raw fruit. If you feel nauseous at the sight of the meal, just take something off the plate containing these nibbles. Never eat anything you don't want, and never have large meals. I want you to eat little and often. It will be made clear that you're on a special diet and no one will question or comment. Carlo understands and will help you.'

He got up and sat close to her on a corner of the desk. Leaning down, he picked up her hand. 'Even if there are problems, my dear,' he said gently, 'life is too precious to throw away. And if you want to talk to me at any time—in confidence—please feel you can do so.'

The buzzer sounded on his desk and he moved round, bending to flick it.

'Don Carlo Vicenzi is here, *dottore*.'

'Please ask him to come in.' He straightened and smiled at her reassuringly as Don Carlo walked in. 'Ah, Carlo, we've just finished.'

'Good.' Carlo's voice was indifferent. 'We have to be going.' The two men shook hands 'Thank you.' Carlo smiled briefly.

Back in the car Rosanna tried to think. She turned her mind resolutely from all the doctor had said, blushing slightly as she remembered that Don Carlo knew all about it. She was determined to have no further intimacy with him. Would he agree to help her prevent their marriage? What would she do if he refused? How could she persuade her grandfather to let her have the money if she didn't marry Don Carlo?

Surely the father of the coming child wasn't important. It was her blood that was needed to provide an Orsini heir.

Don Carlo parked the car. He unlocked the heavy, iron-railed glass door and the express lift which whisked them straight up to the penthouse floor. Rosanna was back in the apartment she had left with such relief the previous day.

'Please go in,' Carlo said coolly, 'I'll let them know we're here.'

The room looked different in daylight, and Rosanna glanced away selfconsciously from the sofa on which she had lain the day before.

'Lunch is all ready.' He led the way through an arch into a second room, and Rosanna had a quick glimpse of a cool arched ceiling, an oval black polished wooden dining table and matching high-backed chairs, before she was through it and outside.

She drew her breath in delight. A large stone terrace sloped gently towards a wide balustrade. Protected from the sun by a trellis of vines climbing across a wooden frame above and cascading down glass walls at the side, the balcony was cool and shady, a glimmer of sunlight flickering through the greenery. She walked to the edge and looked down at the city below, a heat haze shimmering above the spires and cupolas. Across the balustrade pots of brilliant red geraniums and flowering cacti spilled their leaves and blossoms to form a garland of colour.

'You like it?' Carlo stood behind her in the open french windows.

'It's beautiful,' she murmured shyly, breathing in the scent of the blossoms. She turned and smiled at him, her eyes wide and dark with delight. For a moment he stood still, his face intent, eyes veiled by dark lashes. Then he walked down to join her.

'The whole verandah can be glassed in and used all through the winter.' He grinned down at her in sudden good humour, and she was conscious of his height she put her head back to look into his face. 'It's a lovely place to sit and do nothing,' he added. Then he turned. 'Now let's have lunch.' He gestured to the round table behind them. As they sat down a woman came out carrying a large bowl which she put on to the table as she beamed at them both.

'Rosanna, I'd like you to meet Christina, who's been with my family on and off since I was tiny.' He grinned at her. 'We're lucky her own children are now grown up and she can return to us to look after you.'

Rosanna saw a round, comfortable woman of middle age with dark hair drawn back into a luxuriant bun, her hands folded across her stomach, steady black eyes regarding her with friendly curiosity.

'I should warn you Christina is a tyrant,' Carlo continued calmly in the same even impersonal tone, 'and we're all terrified of her. You, too, will be frightened before the week is out into doing exactly what she dictates.'

Christina chuckled. 'The Signor Conte is pleased to joke, but we do not wish to frighten the *signorina* as it is her first visit to Sicily, isn't it?' She fussed over the table, moving a glass, adjusting the angle of a knife. 'I'll leave you now to have your meal in peace . . . and alone,' she ended with an arch smile.

Rosanna blushed, but Carlo wasn't in the least put out. 'You'll have to be careful, Christina,' he said dryly, 'the *signorina* speaks perfect Italian and understands everything you say.'

Christina stopped in the doorway. 'And so I should hope,' she said forcefully, 'is she not marrying a

Sicilian?' And she departed with a quiet laugh.

Rosanna noticed a plate with nuts, figs and grapes at her place. She flushed deeply, recalling her session with Dr Albini. Presumably Christina, too, had been told of her illness.

'Soup?' Carlo asked politely.

'A little, please.'

Unlike most people, he realised she meant a little and poured her just one ladle full of the clear consommé, the *pasta in brodo*, that her mother used to make. It was delicious and they ate in silence. Carlo took bread and helped himself to each course presented. Rosanna took only what she wanted, picking some shrimps, a slice of salami and a few glossy black olives from the *antipasto*, the hors d'oeuvre. He seemed quite content to eat while she nibbled. No one remarked that she didn't touch the *fettuccini* in their rich garlic and tomato sauce, and for the first time since her arrival in Sicily she felt at ease, problems for the moment banished from her thoughts.

Christina brought coffee and left them. Don Carlo got up and lit a slim cigar, standing with his back to her at the balcony edge.

'The English doctor's report on your health was very inadequate,' he said at last. 'No mention was made of your diet problem. Did Albini talk to you about it?'

'Yes.'

'It seems if you follow his instructions, this shouldn't harm the baby.'

'I want to talk to you about that,' she began hurriedly, and found her tongue suddenly sticking to the roof of her mouth. Gallantly she went on as he turned to face her, making her feel even more nervous. 'I c-c-can't go through w-with the m-marriage,' she managed at last. 'I hope you'll agree,' she sighed as her tongue returned to normal, 'that we tell my grandfather it's not possible after all.'

He frowned heavily, apparently deep in thought. 'Do I make you nervous,' he asked, 'that you stutter?'

'I stammer sometimes,' she replied more firmly, 'it's ... I stammered as a child and it comes back sometimes when I ... I'm with people I don't know.'

He narrowed his eyes until they appeared almost closed, but she could feel the tension of his gaze on her face. 'And when did you decide to back out of your contract?' he asked quietly, that hint of menace back in the soft tones of his voice.

'Don't you agree ... it's not possible to go through with it ... with the ... er ... plan?' she asked nervously.

'I'm committed to fulfil a contract and have no intention of backing out. Nor do I envisage your doing so.'

'I'm sorry,' Rosanna said miserably, 'I thought we might agree.'

'Do I understand your decision was made when we met this morning?' he asked harshly.

She got up. 'There's no need to discuss it further,' she said coldly. As yesterday his arrogance cleared her head, dispelling confusion. 'I'll see my grandfather.' She turned to go.

'Just a moment,' he commanded. She stopped and looked back at him.

'Your grandfather won't see you,' he stated flatly.

'Why not?' she asked, her chin rising at the presumption of his words.

'Because he and I have agreed it won't be necessary. I'm in charge of all the arrangements.' He paused. 'Everything,' he stressed.

Rosanna waited. 'I see,' she said finally, 'well, the arrangements will have to be changed. If I wish to see him, I'll certainly do so.'

He was leaning back casually and exhaled a puff of smoke, concealing his expression. 'Perhaps I haven't made myself clear,' he went on deliberately. 'I'm in full charge of all the financial arrangements. We are to be married in four days, when the first sum of money will be despatched to your solicitors in England.' He straightened up. 'Naturally, if the marriage doesn't take place, your solicitors will receive a notice sueing for breach of contract and demanding back the money already expended on your behalf.'

There was a sudden silence and Rosanna felt nausea contract her throat. But she wouldn't give in to his blackmail. 'It's up to my grandfather to make that decision,' she said heavily.

'Very well.' He moved quickly, with the ease of a trained athlete. In two strides he was at her side, and she had a quick vision of his actions yesterday. She stepped back and put her hands up in fear as if to ward him off. Carlo stopped quite still, his jaw visibly clenched. 'Please come with me,' he said tautly, and moved past her into the flat.

Rosanna waited for the heat to recede from her face. What did he mean, he was in charge? Was it up to him what happened to her? Had her grandfather left her completely to Don Carlo's whims? She pulled herself together and followed him.

In the living room he was on the phone, speaking in rapid italian. 'Signorina Dunham wishes to speak to her grandfather,' he was explaining. '*Un momento.*' He handed her the receiver.

'*Pronto*? . . . Signorina Dunham?' She didn't recognise the voice. 'This is Mario Santorini. We met yesterday—I'm your grandfather's private secretary. I'm so sorry, but *il signore* has left Palermo.'

Rosanna bit her lip in vexation. 'When will he return?' she asked. 'It's urgent that I see him.'

'He's gone for the summer, *signorina*. He always does so at this time. We don't expect him back.'

There was silence on the line. 'Would you please give me his address?' she asked next. 'I have to contact him.'

'I am so deeply sorry, *signorina*, but I cannot do so. You understand, I have my instructions. But if there is difficulty, please ask the Signor Conte. He will do everything just as your grandfather would wish.'

Rosanna breathed in deeply. 'Thank you'. She hung up.

'Sit down, Rosanna,' the voice came from behind her. 'Let's discuss this sensibly.'

She sat away from him. Don Carlo stood by the window his back to her. He had the whip hand, the freedom to dictate to her, and she didn't know what to do next.

Suddenly he spoke. 'I've told your grandfather there could be only one reason to cancel the contract,' he said quietly. She raised her head, sudden hope stirring her mind. 'We Sicilians are realists in all things. It's not possible for two people to make a child if they find each other—physically incompatible.' He paused for a moment and then went on smoothly, his drawl pronounced. 'In spite of your youthfulness, I'm aware, as is your grandfather, that you're not an innocent. So you must know if you find me—repulsive ... as a man.' He waited for her to speak. 'If that is so,' he continued after a moment's silence, 'the contract is automatically terminated.'

Rosanna rushed into speech. 'And what happens

then? What do I do? Is there someone else who can
. . . take over? Do I still get the money?'

He stiffened and she realised she had angered him.
Slowly he turned to face her. 'You haven't answered
my question, Rosanna. Do you find me repulsive?'

She noticed his face in the light from the window,
grim and set in anger, the jaw clenched as she had seen
it yesterday.

'I can't answer that, and I don't wish to,' she said
slowly, her face flushing.

'Nevertheless you have to answer. Unless you do,
we go ahead as planned.'

She turned away from him. 'Yes,' she whispered, 'I
do. I'm sorry.'

'If it's true, there's no reason to be sorry. It's a
matter of chemistry. No one is to blame.' He paused.
'If it's true,' he stressed.

She looked across at him. 'What arrangements will
be made now?' she asked anxiously.

'Just a moment. Not so fast,' he said softly. 'First
we have to see if it's true.'

'No . . . please . . . that's not necessary. My word
should be enough.'

Carlo looked at her carefully as she stood on the
other side of the room, his eyes going from her face
down the slender throat to the full, high breasts, the
small waist and the hint of rounded, feminine hips to
the length of slim legs. 'Who knows,' he drawled 'I
may feel the same.' He started towards her. 'If it's
mutual, your grandfather has empowered me to make
other arrangements.'

'What other arrangements?' Rosanna's voice rose
eagerly.

'You really do want to get out of this, don't you?' he
demanded, and she dropped her eyes. 'Well, we'll see.

The test will only take a moment.' He moved nearer and she backed away in fright, her hands stretched out to him, pleading.

'Not this way, please! You must . . . I mean, please take my word for it. You said yourself I do know what I feel. Please. . . .'

He took her outstretched hands in his, pressing them against his chest sliding his arms round her back. Looking down into her eyes now swimming with unshed tears, his own brilliant and hard, he drew her towards him. His eyes moved to her mouth and he bent his head.

Rosanna's heart was hammering with fear as his lips touched hers, his mouth moving lightly against hers. She almost sobbed with relief at the unexpected gentleness of his touch and moved away to free herself, thankful the experiment was over. But his hold on her tightened and his arms pulled her back.

'No, Rosanna,' he murmured, 'you must convince me. Come, little one,' he taunted softly, 'convince me.'

'Once more he bent his head to her mouth, and she stood still in his embrace, determined to show him no response, remaining rigid and cold at his touch. This time his kiss opened her lips to explore and arouse, and suddenly she shivered. No one had ever kissed her so intimately, and unreasoning panic gripped her. She began to fight to free herself, battling to get away, but only succeeded in rousing him to passion. His hands travelled down her back, caressing the curve of waist and hips, his heart thudding against her throat as his kiss hardened demandingly.

Gradually her will-power seemed to melt in the heat between them, and her lips began to respond, her own deeply buried passions flaming into life. Desire engulfed her senses and she kissed him back, ardently.

Eyes closed, no thoughts intruded as excitement raced through her body and she lifted her hands to encircle his neck, her fingers in the crisp silk of his hair.

And then suddenly she was free. His arms dropped and he stepped back from her so suddenly she almost fell on top of him. The blood was drumming in her ears and her thoughts whirled chaotically as she pressed her hands against the cool wall behind her, fighting to remain upright, her legs threatening to buckle. She turned away from him, her breathing heavy in the silence, the heat in her face gradually subsiding.

Intent on herself, she didn't see him turn and pick up a cheroot. Lighting it, he inhaled deeply and then sat down in the nearest chair, his eyes veiled, the lashes dark against the sudden pallor of his face. 'Sit down, Rosanna,' he said coolly, 'before you fall down.'

She groped awkwardly to a chair and sat numbly, unable to think, trying to regain her composure.

'Well, that does seem to solve one problem, doesn't it?' Carlo drawled.

'No,' she whispered, 'you don't understand. A kiss doesn't mean anything.'

'That's a surprisingly cynical view,' he commented lightly, 'but I agree—a kiss means very little. But at least we know each other a little better, don't we?' he asked, mocking.

Rosanna sat silent and miserable, quite unable to understand what had just happened to her. All reason, all willpower had deserted her, and she felt shamed and helpless as she recognised how she had responded to his touch. The few young boys who had fumbled with her clothes at parties and tried to kiss her in the dark had found her cold and contemptuously uninterested. She had accepted that she was unable to respond to any man. And now this arrogant Sicilian, a complete stranger, had managed to prove her wrong. Only his skill and experience of women could account for it. Perhaps any man could make any woman respond if he was sufficiently expert.

'Come, Rosanna, we have a lot to get through,' Carlo's voice intruded into her thoughts, 'and it's getting late.'

Still she sat, sunk in her own speculations, unable to concentrate on what she should do next. Then the matter was taken out of her hands. He got up and came towards her.

'Stand up.'

Weakly she stood before him, not looking into his face, her gaze pinned to the silk shirt through which she could just see the shadow of dark hair that she had felt only moments earlier pressing against her.

Carlo picked up her left hand and slid a ring on to the third finger. The thin gold band with its cluster of diamonds was loose. 'Since you're half English,' he said, 'I thought you'd like an engagement ring, and I've picked this out from the family jewels.'

Rosanna took her hand away from his and the ring dropped off on to the floor. Carlo bent to pick it up.

'Your fingers are even smaller than I guessed.' As he straightened she looked at him and marvelled at his composure, the cool indifference of his voice. It had meant nothing to him—just an experiment. She wondered if all women meant so little. She had listened to stories her mother told of Sicilian men who were proud and passionate, adored their wives, but thought nothing of keeping mistresses that were changed with the seasons.

He caught her glance on him and looked down into her face, pale and shadowed, the mouth full and vulnerable, passion still lingering in the deep dark eyes. For a moment he didn't move, and they looked at each other, speculating, withdrawn, revealing nothing of themselves.

Then he took her hand and led her to the sofa. She didn't resist, and he released her as they sat down. From the little finger of his right hand he drew a ring. It was a signet ring of red gold, curiously worked into a knot in the centre of which glowed a deep blue lapis lazuli. Carlo took her left hand and slid it on to the third finger. It fitted perfectly, and Rosanna looked down at it slightly bemused.

'My friends will recognise it and we'll explain it as a sentimental gesture,' he said quietly. 'It suits you.' He got up. 'If you want a show diamond later I can always buy you one,' he added carelessly.

At that her head shot up, her mind cleared. 'I don't want a ring, thank you,' she said coldly, 'and since I won't be meeting your friends, what they think isn't important.'

He stopped pacing and looked down at her. 'You're going to stop this childishness, Rosanna,' he drawled softly. 'It isn't befitting in my bride. The ring on your finger will remain there.' She was pulling at it, unable to dislodge it. 'As for my friends, certainly you'll meet them. Tomorrow night we are being given a betrothal dinner by my sister-in-law, Maria Vicenzi. She is my brother's widow and will introduce you to the family, to whom we'll present the picture of a happy engaged couple. No one aside from your grandfather and Albini knows the circumstances of our engagement. I've explained that we've been meeting in England where I go on business.' He glanced at his watch. 'And now we must go. Please tidy yourself.'

She stood up, tense and mutinous. 'You're mistaken. My contract doesn't include socialising with your family or appearing in public with you. We marry and I have the child, but I'm not setting up as your wife, socially or in any other way.'

'Do you know, almost you make me angry?' Carlo said mildly. 'You're nothing but a wilful child.' His voice hardened. 'You will behave as any prospective Sicilian bride—that means meeting my family and friends. We'll be invited and in time will return those invitations. And you will be present whenever I wish it—and you'll be dressed for the occasion,' he added, glancing down contemptuously at her dress, his voice arrogant and supercilious. 'Nor do I propose to argue with you over every little aspect of our lives. Kindly remember that I hold the money you're making out of this, and we can both be thankful it'll be at most a year before you return to your own country. While you're my fiancée and my wife, your only object will be to please me, as it would be if you were truly a Sicilian bride of my choice.' He looked into her stormy eyes, his own face cool and indifferent, no sign of anger.

There was a long silence. Rosanna bit back the savage torrent of words that she longed to hurl at him. He had the power to force her to do as he wished. He controlled the money and she had no doubt he would withhold it ruthlessly if he chose.

She bit her lip. For the moment she had to give in. But there had to be an escape; sooner or later she would find a way. No one was going to rule her for long!

She walked ahead of him out of the room.

CHAPTER FOUR

'*SIGNORINA!*'

Rosanna opened her eyes and sat up. She had fallen asleep on the lounger beside the pool, and she blinked for a moment at Sophia, hesitating in the doorway.

'Yes, what is it?'

'*Scusi, signorina*, you have a visitor.'

'Visitor?' Rosanna echoed, bewildered.

'*Si, la* Signora Vicenzi.'

'Signora Maria Vicenzi?'

'*Si.*'

Carlo's sister-in-law.

'Please tell the *signora* I will be with her in ten minutes,' she commanded coolly, 'and offer refreshments.'

'*Si, signorina.*'

Rosanna got up, the sleek black swimsuit showing the creamy skin of her arms and legs. Picking up a brilliant emerald towelling coat, she belted it round herself and made her way upstairs, curious to know what Maria Vicenzi could want, since they would be meeting later that evening at the betrothal dinner she was giving for Carlo and herself.

Rosanna hadn't seen Carlo since the previous afternoon when he had handed her over to Valentina Massima at her salon.

'Here she is,' he had announced casually to the brilliantly beautiful woman, who had kissed him on the mouth, her lips lingering against his. Sleek black hair, olive complexion and large dark eyes, she was round forty, a superb, tall voluptuous figure, exquisitely dressed. Dragging her eyes from Carlo's darkly compelling face, the woman had taken his arm and surveyed Rosanna, who stood awkwardly in the doorway.

'Oh, *caro*,' she had laughed lightly, her glance running over Rosanna's figure, 'no ... even I cannot be the magician here. She is so thin and pale! I have nothing ready—and you want it all so quickly. You understand ...' she looked meltingly into his face, 'I do have other customers,' she purred, laying soft hands with purple-tipped nails lightly against his sleeve.

'Come, Valli, I'm counting on you,' he said gently, the steel in his quiet voice, 'but first let me introduce you. Rosanna Dunham, my fiancée ... Rosanna, this is Valentina Massima, my good friend and the creator of the most beautiful clothes in all Palermo.'

The creator of other things besides clothes, Rosanna thought dryly, looking at them both. There was an intimacy between them she could sense from where she stood across the room. 'It's not necessary for the *signora* to bother with me,' she said coldly, 'I'm well able to find my own clothes.' And she turned to leave.

'Rosanna.' Carlo didn't raise his voice, but in a moment he was at her side, looking down into her face, a smile of genuine amusement in his eyes. 'Come, *piccola*, you mustn't mind Valli. She is outspoken, as you are yourself.' He took her hand and drew it through his arm. 'Alas, I must leave you. As always, Valli, I trust you completely. Something special for tomorrow night, and the rest I leave to you. But please, I want everything—hair, make-up, accessories. Oh, and don't change her,' he smiled down at Rosanna caressingly. 'I like her the way she is. Just give her the clothes to show off her beauty.'

Rosanna blushed furiously. How dared he treat her like a prized possession in need of polish! Looking up into his face, she saw the mocking glow in those cold eyes, dead to all feeling except the arrogant assumption that everyone would always do what he wanted. She lifted her chin and gazed back at him with scornful contempt. He took the chin and held it firmly between two fingers. 'Now, little one,' he asked softly, 'you do want to do me credit, don't you?'

She opened her mouth to tell him exactly what she wanted, but he bent his head swiftly and kissed her hard on her parted lips. With a quick *'Arrivederci'* and a polite bow to them both, he disappeared.

The two women looked at each other. Then Valentina Massima laughed, a natural, gay laugh without a sting. Come, *cara*,' she gestured, 'we'd better get started.'

Rosanna stiffened. 'It's not necessary, *signora*,' she said coldly. 'I'll leave you to make your explanations to Don Carlo. I'm quite able to choose my own clothes. In fact I'd prefer it that way.'

'Now you are being insulting. No one could choose better for you than I. And tomorrow night all Palermo will know you have been dressed by La Massima.'

She took Rosanna's arm and walked her to the back of the showroom. 'You mustn't be jealous of me, *cara*,' she said lightly. 'Carlo and I go back a long way, but it means nothing now. I saw your eyes, how they flashed at our greeting.'

Rosanna was furious. 'You are mistaken, *signora*. I have no interest in him as a man and wouldn't be able to feel jealousy.'

The older woman stared in amazement. 'Are you

mad, child, to talk so? You cannot know what you're saying. All Palermo has been told this is the romance Carlo has been waiting for all his life. He has courted you for a year and you are to be married in less than a week. And you say you don't care for him! Are you marrying him for his money, then?'

Rosanna bit her lip and flushed in embarrassment. She must learn to guard her tongue. 'No, of course not,' she said shortly.

'Ah, you go red. It's not true, of course. Do you know there are hearts breaking because he has found you? Many women have tried and failed where you have succeeded, and you will find much envy. You're lucky he has chosen you, and tomorrow night everyone will look at you to find out why.' Valentina paused. 'That's why he's brought you to me. In my clothes they will know why he has chosen you.' She drew aside the curtains of the fitting room and took Rosanna's hand. 'Now take off your clothes so that we can look at you without that terrible dress.'

Rosanna clenched her hands, controlling her anger with difficulty. She wanted to shout at this woman that she had saved for months to buy the material for the dress she was wearing, and that her mother had sewn it by hand because they had no machine. '*Signora*, I would rather leave now,' she said evenly. 'I understand how busy you are and I'll explain to Don Carlo that it was I who chose to leave. No blame will attach to you.'

'Sit down,' Signora Massima ignored Rosanna's words. 'I think we must have a little talk.' She sat Rosanna in front of the triple mirror and looked at her gravely. 'First of all,' she said quietly, 'please call me Valli. All my friends do, and I hope we're going to be friends. I see from your face that you have spirit, and that I admire. But there's something weighing you down, a sadness and trouble in your eyes which is not right for a girl of your years who is to be married.' Rosanna dropped her eyes and the *signora* continued, 'I do not pry, you understand, but I know Carlo ... from long ago. He has had much unhappiness in his life, much trouble. I wish him a good marriage with a wife who adores him and puts his happiness first. For many years his friends have thought he will never marry again because. ... Oh, he has played, of course,' she went on quickly. 'He is virile, handsome and he is Sicilian. But no marriage—no children. Those of us who care for him have been worried. And now there is you. And I hope he will be lonely no longer, and there will be children. He's due for some happiness.'

She began to unzip Rosanna's dress. Carlo had been married before! That had never been mentioned. Nor had her grandfather informed her.

'I don't know you,' the *signora* continued, 'but you have the chance to be very happy. Take it. And don't look back.' She slipped the dress over Rosanna's head, leaving her with only her bra and briefs. Valli drew a sharp breath.

'Yes,' she breathed, her interest caught. 'Now I see why he's chosen you. That skin! No Sicilian has such skin. And you're young and slender, a beautiful woman in bud.'

And suddenly she snapped into action. 'Marisa!' she called. 'Lucia ... *pronto* ... at once!'

After that Rosanna had no part to play. She felt like a doll as she was measured, prodded and turned. Linens, chiffons, silks, satins and organza were draped on her body for swimwear, underwear, sportswear, shoes, coats, dresses and suits, all colours of the rainbow. Rosanna found her head swimming long before Valli called a halt.

'Are you excited?' the girls demanded eagerly.

'I'm sorry,' Rosanna admitted, 'but I'm not interested in how I look or what clothes I wear.'

Open-mouthed, the women stood round her and stared. At last Valli spoke, her voice incredulous. 'I feel, *cara*, someone has invented you. You can't be real flesh and blood!'

At that Rosanna suddenly put her head back and laughed, loud and clear. Everyone stood stock still, gaping at the transformation in her face. then Valli pounced.

'Now I know what you're wearing tomorrow night,' she said triumphantly, 'and you'll be a sensation!'

Rosanna tied the sash of her tailored white shift and slipped into matching kid sandals. A quick comb through her hair and she was ready to face her visitor.

Her heels clicked on the marble tiles as she crossed the hall to the morning room. At the far end of the room french windows were open to the early evening breeze, the light soft and balmy.

She stopped inside the door and looked at her visitor. Sitting in an upright silk-embroidered chair, Maria Vicenzi was tiny. A generously curved figure with delicate legs and feet, she was dressed formally in a suit of lemon crêpe silk, jewellery in her ears, at her wrists and on her fingers. Her heavy coil of black hair seemed to weigh down the head with its finely arched brows, small mouth and narrow forehead, the symmetry of the face only slightly marred by the rather large, long nose.

At Rosanna's approach she looked up with round

brown eyes that stared unblinkingly, and stretched out a hand in greeting.

'Rosanna,' she said pleasantly as though she were the hostess, 'come and sit down.' She looked Rosanna over carefully as the younger girl pulled up a chair and sat opposite. 'You probably wonder why I've come,' she began, 'but I feel it's important that we have a little chat before this evening—to put you in the picture.'

'It's kind of you to call,' Rosanna said politely.

Maria Vicenzi nodded, inclining her head slightly in acknowledgment of the courtesy. There was an awkward pause and Rosanna wondered why in fact she had come.

'I'm sorry Carlo isn't here,' she hazarded. 'I'm sure he would have wished to introduce us.'

'Has Carlo told you about me?' Maria asked. Rosanna looked at her, eyes questioning. 'I mean has he told you of our plans?' Still Rosanna didn't say anything. 'Perhaps I'd better explain,' Maria went on nervously. 'You know of course about his wife . . . how she died?'

Rosanna refused to be drawn. 'If you'll give me some idea of what I can do for you, *signora*. . . .'

'Oh, please,' the other woman interrupted, 'call me Maria. After all, we're going to be sisters . . . for a time, anyway,' she finished archly. Rosanna stiffened. 'I know, of course, all about the marriage and the . . . er . . . terms.'

Rosanna hid her surprise. Carlo had told her only two people knew of the marriage contract, and Maria had not been one of them.

'You see,' Maria went on smoothly, 'Carlo and I tell each other everything. We're very close.' She looked away, blushing slightly, and then went on in a rush. 'I was married to his brother, did you know that?'

'Yes.'

'And did you know it was Carlo I wanted to marry?'

'We haven't discussed his past,' Rosanna said truthfully.

Maria sighed. 'I was the oldest sister and I had to marry the elder brother. Even though Luigi was the oldest by only half an hour.'

Rosanna drew an audible breath. Carlo was a twin!

Maria paused, a look of triumph on her face. 'You didn't know they were twins? Not identical, of course, and not at all alike in character, but very close, as twins sometimes are. Anyway, my younger sister, Giovanna, married Carlo and I married Luigi. It was all arranged by our parents, of course, and once we were married, Carlo behaved to me only as a brother. Our ... deeper feelings for each other had to be ... er ... hidden.' She coughed delicately. 'But then my husband died and so did my sister, and Carlo and I found each other again.' She sighed extravagantly.

Rosanna wished the other woman would get to the point of this visit. She had no interest in the Vicenzi family history or Maria's feelings for her brother-in-law.

'Unfortunately family interests have to come first once more,' Maria went on. 'You see, I can't have children.' She blushed fiery red and looked at Rosanna earnestly for a moment. 'Since there's no Vicenzi hier, your grandfather's contract came at a good moment for us. Once Carlo has a son we can be married and I will then bring up his child.'

Rosanna sat stunned. Of all the reasons why Carlo would agree to their marriage, this would never have occurred to her.

'I'm telling you all this,' Maria continued, 'so that you understand from the beginning that Carlo is not ... er ... free, that his feelings are engaged ... elsewhere. I wouldn't want you to be misled—hurt. I mean ... please don't hope he'll fall in love with you and want to keep you here once you've had the baby.' Hard eyes stared defiantly at Rosanna. 'I think it's best to be open and honest about these things.'

'I'm not sure I understand,' Rosanna said politely. 'Surely whatever my feelings about Carlo, now or in the future, if he loves you, you've nothing to fear from me.'

A deep flush rose under Maria's dark skin and her small mouth set angrily. 'You know very well what I mean, Rosanna. You're not a child. Carlo is a virile and attractive man. A wife has ... opportunities to persuade and influence ...' her voice tailed away.

'You must forgive me,' Rosanna said quietly, 'if I don't share your candour. My feelings and my marriage are private and concern only my fiancé and myself.'

The hiss of Maria's indrawn breath sounded loud in the quiet room. 'You're insulting, Rosanna, and I can see I'm wasting my time coming here to be nice to you. It's obvious you're cold and unfeeling. You don't appreciate my confidence.'

Rosanna contained her anger. 'I'm sorry I can't give you the assurances you want. They aren't mine to give.'

Maria stood up, her body tense with anger and dislike. 'You'll regret this, Rosanna. You know nothing about Sicilian men,' she said heatedly, 'and your childishness won't help you with Carlo. He's a difficult man and can be heartless and cruel. I've seen it with women who throw themselves at him. For them he has nothing but contempt. Oh, he takes them,' she jeered 'why not? But they cannot reach him, and in the end all he gives them is a trinket, a jewel. But I do understand him, and I could have helped you with him. Well, you've had your chance. But kindly remember it is I who will be his wife for the rest of our lives—the Contessa Carlo Vicenzi,' she finished arrogantly.

'In that case,' Rosanna said quietly, determined not quarrel with Carlo's sister-in-law, 'there's no need for you to worry about me. Probably I, too, will end up with only a trinket.'

She watched Maria Vicenzi as she walked out of the room.

Two hours later, in the same room, Rosanna waited for Carlo. The evening ahead loomed rather threatening, and she wondered what further tensions and problems were in store.

Walking restlessly up and down, she caught sight of herself in the gold framed mirror. Certainly Valentina Massima had done marvels. Her hair had been shortened and lay thick and heavy, cut cleverly to curl softly under her chin, the suggestion of a silky fringe sweeping lightly across her forehead emphasising the depth of her eyes. The lightest make-up only moistened her lips and shadowed her lids.

The dress itself was amazing, and Rosanna marvelled at Valli's daring in choosing it for her. A deep wild rose colour, it was of featherweight crêpe, held up by two narrow diamanté-studded straps. Moulded to the figure, it flared from the hips to fall in loose folds to her feet. Matching high-heeled sandals with diamanté-embossed heels finished the outfit, her only jewellery the deep blue and gold of Carlo's ring.

In the last day some of the tension had faded from her face, the tiredness from her eyes. She had slept deeply during the night and dozed lightly by the pool for most of the day.

It was strange, she thought, that she found no satisfaction in her reflection. Other women would be excited, pleased, flattered to see themselves in the truly magnificent dress. But as she looked into the mirror, she saw only the face of her mother, wan, unhappy and ill. And she felt a fraud, dressed to parade herself for a man who was a stranger and people among whom she didn't belong.

She jumped nervously as the bell rang and Carlo's quiet, deep voice mingled with Sophia's in the silent villa.

He came into the room and stood in the doorway. He was in evening dress, the white jacket emphasising the darkness of skin and hair, the power of that patrician head. Finely tailored black trousers with the old-fashioned silk stripe down the side revealed the length of muscular leg.

He didn't move, his eyes on her, and suddenly she was strangely glad at the way she looked, somehow a match for him for the first time. His gaze went from the top of her ash-blonde hair shining under the lights of the chandelier down to the pink varnish of her toes gleaming faintly through the silk on her sandalled feet.

Sudden emotion flared in the intense blue of his

eyes, but a moment later it had gone, and he bowed ironically.

'Good evening. Rosanna. I see you came to terms with Valli,' he commented softly. 'I must congratulate her on your appearance.'

How true, she thought. He was not complimenting her, but her creator. That was exactly how she felt, as though someone had created her. She smiled grimly, wondering what this coming year would do to her. Would she lose herself completely in the trappings of a stranger? Perhaps never to find her true self again? Such speculation, she knew, was childish. She had to face reality, and reality was the man standing opposite.

'Have I said something amusing?' he asked, raising one eyebrow at her.

'It was nothing—just a thought. Is it time to go?'

'In a moment.' He slipped his hand into his pocket and took out a flat box. As he opened it he walked towards her. 'I've brought you a present and I want you to wear it tonight. It should go well with that dress.'

He pulled out a necklace and held it up for her to see. A web of sparkling diamonds intricately set into antique silver with a clear-cut diamond pendant hanging from it like a huge pearl. Rosanna caught her breath, as the light from the chandelier struck the blue and white fire of the stones. She had never seen a precious stone, but there was no mistaking it.

'Come, let me put it on.'

'No!' Her voice was adamant. 'I don't want it,' she said rudely, then pulled herself up. 'I mean . . . I don't want to wear it. It's too valuable. I might lose it.'

'I wonder, Rosanna, do you ever use the simple

word "yes"? Your answer to everything seems to be no.' Carlo moved to stand behind her. 'Now,' he said softly, 'look into the mirror while I put it on.'

Abruptly she moved away from him. 'Please . . . I really don't want it. I never wear jewellery, and I feel silly enough dressed up like this without adding fairytale trimmings.'

'I begin to despair of you,' he said quietly. 'Have you nothing of the woman in you? You are all childish resentment and rebellion. It doesn't become you, Rosanna. Try smiling and saying thank you—perhaps it's not as difficult as you think.'

He had put her in the wrong again, as though wishing to be independent of him was a whim, a caprice. 'I'm not childish!' she retorted heatedly. 'Why can't you understand that I won't become a puppet to serve you as a Sicilian slave?'

'I can see you're feeling much better,' he commented gravely, and clasped the necklace round her neck. 'There—now look at it. Really look, and recognise its beauty.'

Rosanna looked into the mirror, meeting his eyes, her own wide with sudden doubt. The necklace looked stunning, and she had to admit he was right: it did suit the dress. Her skin seemed to glow with the delicacy of the dress and the fire of the diamonds.

'Thank you,' she said quietly. 'I mustn't forget to return it to you at the end of the evening.'

'Good grief, girl, can't you accept it as a present? It's yours, and I don't care a damn what you do with it after tonight. As long as you don't send it to the lover who's getting all the money you're earning with me,' he finished irritably.

She gasped. 'What do you mean?'

'You heard me,' he said harshly, his voice for once

losing its drawl. 'Only a lover desperate for money could make you go through with such an arrangement.' His lips curled contemptuously. 'It's not surprising you can't bear the beauty of dress and jewels, when you hold your womanhood so cheap.'

The silence seemed to stretch between them while Rosanna tried to understand what he had said. He thought she was doing this for money to send to a lover! Why? How could he think such a thing? She felt suddenly sick and her hand went to her throat to still the rapid movement of her pulse. As her fingers touched the cold of the necklace, her weakness subsided.

'How dare you!' she exclaimed, her voice rising in anger. 'You know nothing about me or my reasons for ... anyway, it has nothing to do with you. Your business is only that I have the child. How easy or difficult that is for me isn't your concern.' She swallowed the lump in her throat. 'If you can't understand how distasteful I find this added charade of dressing up and pretending to feelings I could never have, then I can't help you. A man of honour and honesty would find it possible to respect my feelings!'

She turned away from him, close to tears, trying to control herself. Carlo's hands came down on to her shoulders, warm against her skin, and he turned her to face him.

'Come, we can't have tears falling on that lovely dress, can we?' he asked quietly, and began mopping them up with a large white handkerchief. When he had finished he continued to hold her firmly between his hands. 'You and I, Rosanna, have to come to an understanding for the time we'll be together. We can't go on like this. You must know from your mother that there are things important to a Sicilian that aren't valued in your country. Family pride comes before all else. Tonight we'll be watched closely by members of my family who know me well. Whether you like it or not they are important to me. I have to go on living among them when you go.' He straightened, dropping his hands from her shoulders, and his voice hardened. 'You will do as I say in the end, and it would be easier for both of us if you accept that.'

His face closed grimly against her, the blue eyes hard, staring coldly down into hers. 'Remember, Rosanna, if you disobey me, it is not I who will suffer. Unless you learn and learn quickly not to fight my authority, the hurt and humiliation will be yours. Don't imagine for a moment you can fight me and win. I always win,' he finished arrogantly, and turned away. 'And now please repair your face. It's time to go.'

The evening Rosanna had dreaded turned out quite differently from her expectations. They were the last to arrive and stood side by side, a tall, slim, handsome couple, a sea of curious faces turned towards them in the vast reception room of the Villa Vicenzi.

'Carlo darling, at last!' Maria floated towards them in black lace, her brilliant red lips matching the rubies at her throat, in her ears and on her fingers. She kissed Carlo on the mouth and linked her arm through his, turning him so that they both faced Rosanna. Carlo introduced them, and the older woman didn't betray by a flicker in her expression that they had met earlier in the day. Rosanna was surprised, but said nothing, merely bowing politely.

After that Carlo remained firmly at her side. Arms

linked, they went round the room, smiling, shaking hands, murmuring greetings, until Rosanna was bemused with uncles, aunts and cousins whose names she knew she would never remember.

In the equally vast formal dining room, its walls draped in red silk, riotous frescoes looking down from the vaulted ceiling, she was separated from Carlo, who was sitting at Maria's right hand at the far end of the huge table.

Listening vaguely to the conversation round her and smiling or nodding when it seemed appropriate, Rosanna looked at Maria Vicenzi. She was very obviously devoting all her attention to her brother-in-law, talking to him, listening raptly to his answers and touching him lightly on the hand, leaning intimately towards him, her voice trilling with delighted laughter.

Looking at Carlo, Rosanna wondered about his feelings. He was certainly responding, talking back. But she could see no passion in his face, no warmth or tenderness for the woman at his side. His face was set grimly as usual, and she wondered if it was boredom that triggered off his withdrawal. In the end it didn't matter to her what he felt for his sister-in-law. It was for them to sort out.

She ate carefully, although she was ravenous, remembering what the doctor had said. But when the dessert arrived, the famous Sicilian *cassata*, a rainbow-coloured ice bombe with nuts and glacé fruit, she was tempted. As she was spooning it into her mouth, the young man at her side addressed her for the first time.

'You look at my sister,' he remarked blandly. 'Do you think her beautiful?'

'Your sister?'

'*Si* . . . I am Antonio Manzini, Maria's little brother,' he explained. 'We were introduced, but you have forgotten.' He waved one hand airily. 'There are too many of us to remember.'

Rosanna smiled at him. He was small and slender, with a sleek cap of black hair close to his head, the same brown eyes as his sister, but with long black lashes. His skin was dark and his upper lip sported a thin moustache, giving him a slightly rakish look. Rosanna liked what she saw.

'You approve?' he asked, smiling brilliantly. 'I hope so, because I certainly approve of you. It's a pity we didn't meet earlier . . . before Carlo found you.' He gestured vaguely to emphasise his point. 'I'm the baby of the family, but I fear I'm not altogether safe for young girls to know.' He leaned towards her, his eyes twinkling. 'But you, Rosanna, a beautiful English rose, fresh and delicate—you're different, I think. Young—innocent, yes, but I feel . . . I hope . . . also with a sense of humour. Am I right?'

Responding to his lighthearted nonsense, her spirits lifted and she smiled back. 'True,' she mocked, 'but sadly my humour only appears in the evening and disappears at the witching hour just before dawn.'

'But that is altogether delightful,' he replied, laughing with her, 'it means we have to spend the night together for you to prove it to me. Ah,' he laughed again as she blushed, 'a hit, you must admit. My round!'

Rosanna put back her head and laughed. He was mad, just what she needed to put her situation into some kind of perspective.

'You see,' he went on darkly, 'how shocked they are at your laughter. It is sunlight and joy and youth. But it's forbidden. In the best circles you don't laugh, *carina*, you're merely amused.' And he pulled a face at her.

Suddenly selfconscious, she looked round to discover several people staring at them both. Her eyes lifted up the table to find Carlo watching her, his face grim, his eyes flashing with anger. Her smile faded and she suddenly wanted no more ice cream.

Maria rose and the ladies left the room, adjourning to the open verandah where coffee and liqueurs were being served. Rosanna walked down the steps into the garden, breathing the cool air, her earlier happier mood of the dinner table gone. She wished passionately that she could go home. As she looked at the palms swaying gently, their spiky leaves outlined against the moonlit sky, her thoughts returned to her mother. Was she missing her, or was she content to be in the idyllic surroundings of the clinic? She wondered if Carlo would allow her to go back to England for a visit once they were married.

She tensed at the sound of approaching footsteps. Was it Carlo come to find her?

'Ah, here you are.' It was Antonio Manzini. 'All alone in the dark?'

She jerked out of her thoughts. 'No,' she said cheerfully, 'just coming in. Too many insects out here.'

He turned back with her. 'Rosanna, if you should wish for company at any time or be in need of a friend, even someone to show you the sights, please let know. If you would permit, I would be most happy to escort you.'

'Thank you,' she said formally, 'I'll ask Carlo what our plans are. There isn't very much time before the wedding.'

'Of course,' he replied, and they mounted the steps to join the others.

Carlo was standing in the shadows of the verandah smoking a cheroot. As she arrived with Antonio he moved towards her and took her hand, his fingers cruelly tight on hers. 'Come, *cara*, there's something I want to show you,' he said smoothly, and drew her into the house. Opening a door from the hall, he ushered her into what looked like a library. Closing the door, he leaned against it in the dark, still holding her hand, and pulled her to stand in front of him.

'What is it, Carlo?' she asked nervously, 'wh-wh-what do you want?'

'You're trying my patience, Rosanna.' He was taut with anger and she could feel it flow over her. 'You're engaged to me. That means you don't flirt with other men, especially a boy whose head you turn till your flattery makes him dizzy and he follows you out into the garden to make love to you. What do you imagine Maria thought?' he demanded harshly. 'Quite apart from what you owe to me, you were unpardonably rude to her!'

Rosanna guessed Maria would be delighted to make trouble, to fan the flames of Carlo's anger. 'Did Maria tell you where I was?' she asked lightly.

'Certainly. It was her duty to do so,' he replied severely. 'She also explained that her brother followed you. She was worried for you because he's ... he hasn't a good reputation with girls and it's a cause of distress to her. But perhaps you're fully aware of what he is and encouraged him to come out after you?'

'You are insufferable, Carlo!' she spat at him, and wrenched her hand to free it from his grasp. But she was helpless against his strength, her wrist limp between his fingers.

'How many more times do I have to tell you you're not in England now, free to dispense your favours where you wish?' His voice grated. 'What else must I do to make you understand?'

'Beat me, perhaps,' she taunted. 'I wouldn't put it past you.' Suddenly she sighed wearily, tired of the whole pointless argument. 'For heaven's sake, Antonio is a boy of my own age! We joked and laughed over dinner, that's all. He's Maria's brother, after all. Do you think he would ever forget I'm engaged to you?'

His hold on her hand slackened and she shook her hand free, rubbing her wrist.

A sudden click and the room was flooded with light. Carlo looked at her and she held his gaze, daring him to disbelieve her. He sighed heavily, sudden tiredness in his face, and moved away from the door.

'Very well, Rosanna, let's leave it at that.'

'Do we go back now?' she asked.

'Not with that tight and angry look on your face,' he said.

'No more tight and angry than yours. Just look in the mirror!' she replied tartly.

'We'd better give them a reason why we left the company, then,' he drawled, and moved towards her.

Rosanna turned and wrenched at the door handle to get out of the room, but he was too quick for her. Grasping her hand, he turned her into his arms. His head swooped and she closed her eyes, held inescapably as his lips found her mouth. He kissed her deeply as he had done the day before, but with passion held in check, his lips leaving hers to move across her eyes, her cheeks to the soft lobes of her ears, gently teasing. Another swift hard kiss on the mouth and she was free. Carlo held her at arms's length looking down into her face.

'You'll do,' he said softly. 'They'll know why we left them.'

'They'll think they know,' she retorted quickly.

'Always the last word, Rosanna?' he drawled mockingly.

'Of course,' she replied lightly as he took her hand, and they made their way back to the party.

CHAPTER FIVE

ROSANNA opened the shutters and walked out on to the balcony, leaving the bedroom behind her in darkness.

Her wedding night. It had been the longest day of her life, and it wasn't over yet. Starting twenty-four hours earlier, she had made a final, desperate attempt to persuade Carlo to return to the civil ceremony as planned, instead of the church wedding he had arranged. The contract had specified a civil ceremony to avoid problems later with the divorce. But Carlo had been adamant. His family, his friends would never believe in the marriage unless it took place in church.

When he had finally left her drained and unhappy, she had felt a real hatred of him for the first time. Bitterly she reflected that Maria was welcome to him, and the sooner she was pregnant the sooner any intimacy between them would end.

Carlo had told her nothing of the wedding arrangements, and it wasn't till she drew up at the church with Maria's father to give her away that she realised she was outside Palermo cathedral. Her path blocked by staring strangers, she walked into the interior of the huge church, its baroque richness a visual feast after the austere exterior. Up the nave and under the dome huge marble columns supported the soaring roof above. It was a church for solemn vows to last a lifetime; instead Rosanna knew she had come to lie and cheat. Unconscious of the crowded pews, she prayed throughout the ceremony only for forgiveness.

When they were pronounced man and wife, she

didn't look at her husband. Her eyes veiled she offered him her cold cheek to kiss.

The reception that followed at the Villa Vicenzi, with its ballroom set out for a grand luncheon for two hundred guests, was an endless ordeal of speeches as one course followed another. The focus of all eyes, Rosanna sat stiffly in her ivory satin dress with Carlo at the top table, smiling mechanically till the muscles of her jaw ached and her throat throbbed with unshed tears.

When at last it was over and they were alone in the car, even Enrico left behind, she was too tired to care about their destination. Carlo had explained that he didn't wish to spend the honeymoon at the family villa on Mondello beach, and Rosanna had wondered if that was where he had gone with Giovanna. Instead, he was taking her along the coast to the small fishing port of Cefalu where he had a house outside the town built high above the rocks overlooking the Aegean Sea.

Arriving in the early evening, Rosanna had taken no notice of her surroundings, going straight to her room where the maid unpacked while she lay in a bath, stiff and tense, tiredness battling with rage. During dinner they chatted politely for the servants, and at the end of the meal she hadn't touched Rosanna excused herself, refusing coffee and going straight up to her room.

And now her rage was spent. She felt exhausted, far too weary in mind and body to feel or think. Even the silence and the cool breeze from the sea was no balm to her mood. She wondered what lay ahead before morning. If she was to become Carlo's wife in fact, at least she would be too tired to suffer much.

'Rosanna?' Carlo had come into the room behind her.

'Yes,' she answered wearily.

'Here you are,' he came out on to the balcony. 'Have you had a rest?' He breathed deeply. 'It's so lovely here, so cool and quiet.' Then he turned to her. 'You must be tired, *cara*—come to bed.'

She walked past him into the bedroom, uncomfortably aware of his short silk robe, wondering rather fearfully if he was wearing anything underneath. He bent to the light and a soft glow lit the room.

'Shall we close the shutters?'

She didn't answer, and he went to pull them shut. The room seemed suddenly intimate and the bed looked enormous. Rosanna shivered as Carlo came up behind her and took off her negligee, leaving her in the lacy nightdress Valli had picked for the wedding night.

'You're tense,' he said quietly. 'Tired?'

She pulled away from him. 'Yes, terribly tired. I think I'd like to go straight to sleep, Carlo, if you don't mind.'

'Oh, but I do mind—very much. Come, *cara*, we've both worn ourselves out in the preamble to this situation, and now's the time to stop talking and relax.'

Silent and numb, she stood with her back to him. He touched her shoulders lightly and turned her round, looking down into her face, pale and deeply shadowed, the eyes hidden below thick lashes. With a short impatient exclamation he bent and picked her up, striding with her to the bed. Then he laid her down and turned off the light.

She shrank from him, edging away to the other side of the bed as she heard him drop his robe and lie down beside her. He reached for her and she cried out in panic.

'Come, Rosanna, this shy innocence has been endearing, but you can drop it now.' His voice was quietly amused as his hands moved over her and he bent his head to her lips. She froze in his arms, unable to respond, her heart pounding with fear.

'For heaven's sake, Rosanna, stop it! We both know how expertly you can respond to me, so do it now. Touch me, help me—you know how.'

She lay rigid, unable to speak, her throat locked, as his voice reached her from the outline of his head, all she could see in the darkness of the room. Her hands were clammy with fear, and she was afraid she would shriek if he touched her again.

She felt him lower his body to her and search with his mouth for her lips, one hand caressing her throat.

At last she found her voice. 'No, please . . . I don't . . . I . . . can't . . . I don't know what to do!' her voice rose hysterically. 'I don't know . . . you'll have to force me . . . I can't. . . .' Her voice sank to a whisper.

She felt him stiffen, then he rolled off her body to the edge of the bed. For a moment he lay there motionless. 'I think you'll have to explain that,' he said at last.

'I . . . it's what I said.' I c-c-can't h-help you. I've never been with a man before.' She sighed with relief as her speech cleared. 'I don't know what to do. You'll have to force me. I'm . . . I'm . . . frigid.' She stopped suddenly as she realised she was babbling, repeating herself.

Carlo bent to the floor for his robe and belted it round himself before reaching for the bedside lamp and switching it on. The sudden light dazzled Rosanna and she put one hand across her eyes. Carlo looked at her for a moment and then got up, his back to her.

'It doesn't make sense,' he said heavily at last. 'If

you've never been with a man before, what makes you think you're frigid?'

'I just know. I . . . I'm quite prepared for you to force me, and I'll try not to resist.'

Suddenly he moved, walking swiftly through the communicating door into the dressing room, and she rolled over, burying her head in the pillow to stifle her cry of relief. He was going to leave her alone.

But in a moment he was back. 'Here, drink this,' he said curtly, and she heard the clink of glasses.

'No, thank you,' she said politely, lifting her head, 'I don't want anything.'

'You need it more than I do. Come on, Rosanna, it's just a small glass of brandy. It'll help you to relax. You'll go into muscle spasm if you don't let up.'

She sat up and accepted the glass. As she put it to her lips, it clattered against her teeth and she began to shiver. Carlo picked up her robe and came round the bed, draping it across her shoulders. Then he took his own glass and sat down in an armchair facing her.

The alcohol stung her throat and she winced as she swallowed, but the spirit spread warmth through her body and her fears receded. She looked across at her husband.

'I'm quite ready to be forced,' she said calmly and seriously.

'For heaven's sake stop saying that!' Carlo was angry, and she wasn't surprised. 'Do you imagine a child of mine is going to be born as a result of my raping his mother?' He drank deeply. 'Even you can't be as ignorant as that!'

She quailed before his anger, unable to meet his eyes.

'Whatever made you embark on anything like this,'

he asked roughly, 'when you'd no experience of men? You must have been mad!' A frown settled between his eyes as he sat there staring at her, his face hard, his eyes inscrutable. 'Who told you you're frigid? That isn't usually something virgins make up.'

Rosanna flushed. 'It was a long time ago and I don't want to talk about it.'

'It can't have been a long time ago. Good heavens, girl, you're only twenty now!'

She said nothing.

'Was it someone you loved who was clumsy?'

'No. Just leave it.' She pulled together the edges of her robe. 'I'll try and ... give you what you want ... need. Isn't that enough?'

Carlo put up a hand and slid it impatiently through his hair, ruffling it into disorder. 'No, it's not enough. You're going to have to tell me sooner or later,' he commented.

'You can't make me,' she said childishly.

'Is it that painful?' he asked quietly.

She remembered it as though it were yesterday, because it came back so often into her memory. She had been lying in bed awake. Fear always kept her awake when her father was out drinking. She'd been dozing off when she heard him. He managed to get his key in the lock, and she heard him lurching upstairs, cursing. Then suddenly her door opened and he stood there, swaying in the doorway. She shrank away from him under the bedclothes hoping he would just go away. But he didn't. He closed the door and came towards her, and overbalanced against the edge of the bed, falling on top of her. She wasn't even sure that he knew who she was. Nearly she called out for her mother, but didn't want to frighten her. Pushing at him, she tried to get away, but he was too heavy for her, and she prayed he would just fall asleep so that she could escape.

Suddenly he began to tear at her nightgown, and she opened her mouth to scream, but he clamped his hand across it. Then he started to feel her all over and tried to make love to her. She had been fifteen at the time and terrified, sick with revulsion, but even more frightened her mother might wake and find them. Silently she fought him, biting, scratching, kicking, till he cursed and she was sure her mother must hear them.

At last she got away, her nightgown ripped, her body scratched. For a moment he seemed to sober up, and stopped threshing around. He turned to her and spoke quite clearly, his mind suddenly free of drink, his eyes empty and unrecognising. 'You frigid little bitch,' he said deliberately, 'you'll never be any good to a man.'

Then he had fallen back on to the bed into a deep sleep, and she had slipped downstairs, shaking with fear, to spend the rest of the night dry-eyed on the sofa. In the early dawn she had crept upstairs to lie in a deep bath, scrubbing her body till it hurt.

'Well?' Carlo interrupted her thoughts. 'I'm your husband, Rosanna, and I'm going to have to know. Who was it?'

She swung her legs round, putting her feet to the ground, sitting on the edge of the bed with her back to him, still holding her glass.

'Who was it, Rosanna?'

'My father,' she said at last, her voice devoid of emotion.

'What happened?'

'I just told you.'

'You haven't told me anything yet.'

'You're bullying me, Carlo and I wish you'd stop. You've no right!'

'Don't sidetrack me with nonsense, Rosanna. Just tell me. It wasn't simple, was it? It wasn't said in anger as a father might say it to his daughter, half joking? Am I right?'

'All right,' she said dully. 'My father was ill.'

'Drunk,' he corrected.

She looked round at him in surprise. 'What do you mean?'

'You don't imagine your grandfather was ignorant of your family problems, do you?' He sighed impatiently. 'So . . .?'

'Yes, well, he drank . . . rather a lot. And when he'd been drinking he sometimes . . . didn't know what he was doing. Then he wasn't responsible for his actions. . . . The next day he wouldn't remember anything about it. My mother suffered because he was often violent with her. But she refused to tell anyone, get help. Sicilian pride!' she said bitterly. 'I know all about it. I was brought up with it.'

'So I touched a raw nerve with that, did I?' he asked softly. 'So. . . .'

'I can't, Carlo!' Her voice was agitated. 'I've never told anyone I can't talk about it. I don't even want to think about it. Please,' she whispered, 'don't make me!'

Carlo was at her side in a moment. Taking the glass from her, he held her hands firmly in his. 'Look at me, Rosanna,' he commanded. She shook her head. 'Look at me,' he repeated angrily. He turned her head towards him and gripped her chin, fingers biting into her soft skin. She winced and closed her eyes. 'Open your eyes and look at me.'

'No,' she answered weakly as the tears fell from her lashes. 'I don't understand why it's so important.'

He let go of her chin and put his hands either side of her face, holding her head gently. Then he bent forward and brushed his lips lightly across her closed eyes and along her temples. The tender touch surprised her and she opened her eyes to find his, intense and dark, looking steadily into hers. 'Come, *cara*, tell me now. Trust me. It'll be like telling yourself,' he murmured, 'and then I'll let you sleep.'

She shuddered. 'One night he came to my room and fell on to my bed. He began to ... touch me, as though. ...' she clasped her hands to her head. 'Oh, no!'

'And what happened, *carissima*? Come, tell me ... it will ease your mind.'

He leaned forward and took her into his arms, cradling her against him as he might a child.

'He started to make love to me and I ... fought him. In the end ... I escaped, and he sort of sobered up suddenly. He looked me straight in the eyes and told me ... he said ... I was a frigid bitch and would never be any good to a man.'

She felt him stiffen against her and heard his indrawn breath. Putting back her head, she looked up into his face. His eyes were blazing with anger. 'Carlo,' she questioned, 'are you angry?'

'No, *cara*, not with you,' he murmured, and leaned forward to stroke her disordered hair away from her face. 'There, little one, it wasn't so difficult, was it?' he asked quietly. Slipping her robe from her shoulders, he laid her back on to the bed and covered her with a blanket. 'Now go to sleep.'

With a small sigh Rosanna put her head into the pillow and closed her eyes. Within moments she was asleep, and didn't see her husband as he looked down at her, the tear-stained face, one hand under her cheek, sleeping like a child. Quietly he turned away, switched off the light and left.

The next morning Rosanna woke as the sun filtered through the shutters. She lay back feeling strangely well, her head clear, her spirits lifted. Turning back the covers, she got up and opened the shutters to the morning air.

Immediately below was a wide terrace shaded by giant cacti planted into stone-edged raised flower beds. Huge spreading plane trees lined the railings of the terrace, and she could see steps leading steeply down to a small beach surrounded on all sides by craggy black rocks throwing their shadows into the deep turquoise of the sea. The water glistened in the early morning sunlight, so clear she could see right down into the thick tangled black of seaweed on the bottom.

Quickly she showered and put on a sundress. Slipping into casual sandals, she made her way downstairs, then stepping out on to the terrace, she looked back at the house. Surprisingly, it was modern, glass-fronted to the sea on all levels, with cunningly designed small terraces to give shade and sunlight as one might wish at any time of day.

Standing by the railings she breathed in deeply, the cool breeze ruffling her hair and tingling against her skin.

'Come on, lazybones, time for breakfast!'

Rosanna turned to see Carlo behind her. He was dressed only in brief white shorts, showing the smooth muscles of shoulders and long legs under the deeply tanned skin, black hair curling on his chest up to his throat. She blushed under his gaze, suddenly recalling the previous night, but he seemed unaware of her confusion.

'Of course,' he drawled, 'I do know how beautiful I am, but if you stare at me all day, we'll both die of starvation!'

She laughed and followed him into the house. To her surprise they crossed the hall and walked down the shallow steps into the kitchen below. Airy and cool, it was large, superbly equipped, and Rosanna could smell coffee percolating on the roomy centre table where breakfast was laid out for two.

Carlo smiled in brilliant good humour, and for the first time she was aware of his charm, the magnetism and the male strength of his lean dark body.

'Bacon?' he asked. 'Eggs? I'm cooking this morning.' And Rosanna watched in amazement as he donned a striped cook's apron and began work with butter, pan and eggs.

'Just coffee and rolls for me,' she answered shyly, and gazed in awe as he made himself an enormous cooked meal.

'I've sent the servants away,' he announced next. 'I thought it would be nice if we looked after ourselves.' He looked round and pointed. 'We've a dishwasher, plenty of food, and we can travel round the house, occupying different rooms each day, moving as one gets dirty to the next. Like,' he snapped his fingers, 'what is that English story?'

'Alice in Wonderland—the Mad Hatter's tea party,' she laughed. 'All you need is the hat and you could be the host!'

He stopped and stood still as they looked at each other in sudden silence.

'It is good,' he said lightly, 'you've rested and your

eyes are clear. Now let's eat—I'm ravenous! I've been swimming while you slept.'

As Rosanna lived through the next days she knew they would be etched in her memory to be savoured later.

Carlo was a changed man from the taciturn, grim stranger she had known during the previous week in Palermo.

They spent their days in swimwear and shorts, lazing on the terraces over meals, sleeping during the heat of the day, and propelling themselves into mad activity in the early mornings and late afternoons.

Carlo taught her to snorkel, and they travelled together under water, marvelling at the sea life round the coast. They sped out of the bay in his powerful, gleaming white motorboat, excitement gripping Rosanna as the spray glistened coolly against her skin, to land on some deserted island inlet where they raced each other across the sands and climbed in sneakers up the rocks to collapse exhausted at the top, drinking in the beauty of sun, sea and sky.

Carlo bought her a huge cartwheel straw hat through which the sun dappled her face. Side by side they would cleave through the clear water together and he would oil her skin when they emerged, his hands light and impersonal on her body. In the day there were odd feather kisses on her nose, and at night he kissed her lips swiftly and hard before he left her at her bedroom door.

And slowly the tensions ebbed from Rosanna's mind and body. She began to relax, feeling strangely secure and protected, finding an easy companionship with her husband that she had never known with anyone.

She ate when she felt like it and they took it in turn

to cook. Sometimes they would stash a picnic in the back of the car and go roaring down the motorway through some silent village and on to a different beach, sitting in the shade of an olive grove, lazily watching the sea lapping the beach, water rippling and foaming over the hot silvery pebbles.

At night they listened to music and found they shared some of the same loves, from classical jazz to light opera. As they lay on loungers, the villa behind them in darkness, the music swelled round them in the cool of the night air, seeming to echo back from the black of the Aegean Sea below.

On the third day Carlo took her to Agrigento. They started off in the heat of the afternoon, arriving outside the town as the shadows darkened and the last of the coaches pulled out from the Valley of the Temples. Leaving the car, they wandered round the deserted Doric temples, and Rosanna was amazed to see some in ruins, crumbling under the double onslaught of heat and earthquakes, and others in various stages of restoration. The temple to Zeus was almost totally destroyed, but the Concord Temple was a living miracle, intact as it was built over two thousand years before when the Greeks had quarried the golden sandstone to create a fitting place of worship to their gods.

Dusk came swiftly and Rosanna sat, pleasantly tired, watching the setting sun strike fiery sparks from the white and gold of stone before sinking beyond the horizon into the sea.

Leaning against a pillar, his tall figure barely visible, Carlo talked to her of Sicily. Throughout history the island had been conquered by every major civilisation, its position in the Mediterranean a focal point for every military commander seeking a base for ships and soldiers, from Hannibal to the Germans of the twentieth century.

Each conquest had left its mark on the island, adding to the priceless heritage of buildings, churches and temples that brought the world to admire and enjoy. But money for preserving the island's monuments and treasures was scarce. Many of Sicily's richest sons were scattered round the world, and Rosanna heard the ring of pride in her husband's voice as he described how a group of Sicilians worked tirelessly to find money and experts to carry out the restoration work that would continue for generations to come. She listened spellbound as she glimpsed another side to her husband, hearing him talk for the first time of something that deeply concerned him, dedicating his time and energy to help the traditions and people of the island home he loved.

The next night they went dancing. He took her to Cefalu, and they walked slowly from the floodlit main cathedral square, its outdoor cafés thronged, through narrow streets down to the port, empty of fishing boats out at sea, their brilliant spotlights dotted beyond the bay.

Arm in arm they wandered to a discotheque where youngsters were dancing under fairy lights strung across an open square. Carlo took her in his arms and they moved slowly to the music. They had both changed, and her long chiffon skirt floated round his black-clad legs, her head resting against the white of his jacket. She felt his body, hard and muscular against hers, his hands round her back as he folded her close. Under her cheek she could hear his heart beating and sudden emotion gripped her. Shutting her eyes, she wondered what this would be like if they were truly husband and wife on their honeymoon. Her throat tightened in sudden pain, and he must have felt her tension. He stopped and held her against him. With a hand under her chin he raised her head, and she closed her eyes, waiting for his kiss.

At the touch of his lips a quiver of response went through her, and his kiss hardened. As on that first day, she kissed him back, but with a deeper excitement. The music stopped and they heard clapping. Looking up, they found themselves alone on the dance floor being enthusiastically applauded.

Rosanna blushed deeply, but Carlo laughed and, holding her to his side, he ordered wine all round before they escaped and returned home.

That night Rosanna had her nightmare. It was always the same. It began in church where she lay in her coffin, trying to get out. She fought, cried out and pounded the box, but no one heard her. Eventually she was lowered into her grave, still screaming, and began to suffocate.

'Rosanna, wake up!' It was Carlo shaking her.

She shuddered, coming back slowly to reality. She was in bed, the light from the dressing room streaming through the open door and Carlo holding her. She began to weep, helplessly, clinging to his robe as sobs racked her body, and he murmured softly to her, stroking her gently till she emerged from the dream.

Slowly she was conscious that the movement of his hands had changed, touching, caressing, fingers trailing down her body over her breasts, the flatness of her stomach and down her thighs, bringing her skin to shuddering response through the satin of her nightdress.

Pushing aside the straps across her shoulders, he bent his head to touch the pulse at her throat, moving his lips across the soft curve of her breasts.

In sudden panic she recoiled from him, arching her body away. 'No . . . no, please. . . .' she moaned.

'Easy, *cara*, easy,' he whispered softly. 'Don't fight it . . . I won't hurt you. Come to me now. . . .'

He bent his mouth hot and hard to her lips, opening them, devouring as passion rose between them, and Rosanna could feel the heat of her body responding to his demands. Carlo slid her nightdress down over her body and lifted his head to gaze down at her, his eyes blazing. Shrugging off his robe, he lay down, his hands and lips on her skin, rousing her slowly to an agony of sensations she had never imagined, till she felt she would explode with emotion, her only desire and longing for closeness with his lean hard body.

She woke to find the door to the next room closed and the shutters open to the dawn light filtering into the room. Carlo bent to kiss her lips, his hands on her, gently demanding, and this time there was no fear. She was eager for the intimate caresses she had feared, and within moments she was roused, her fingers shyly exploring, till he groaned his pleasure and took her with him on a tide of passionate joy and wanting, and she thrilled to his cry of pleasure before she collapsed into sleep in his arms.

Rosanna woke to sunlight touching her face, alone in the vast bed. Stretching languorously, she turned her face into the pillow as memory of the night returned and her face suffused with colour.

Never had she imagined such happiness. One night out of her life, yet she felt wholly changed, aware of her body with a new, rapturous self-confidence. She was capable of loving a man and being loved in return, being wanted and desired. Her husband. Her face glowed as she remembered the touch of his mouth and hands, the feel of the satin-muscled skin under her fingers and the weight of his body against her.

It seemed incredible that yesterday they had been strangers, and now they were in love. It had to be love, this sense of fulfilment, this miracle of feeling that had shattered her defences and brought her to her first knowledge of closeness with a man. Carlo hadn't actually mentioned love, but his body had spoken the emotions he hadn't expressed.

She flung back the sheets and got up, looking at herself in the shower, marvelling that there was no visible sign of the emotions of the night. Brushing her hair till her scalp tingled, she dressed in a mint sundress, the tan of her shoulders showing up the gold of her hair bleached by the sun, her eyes almost violet with the glow of happiness.

The house was silent, but she knew where to find Carlo and ran lightly down to the kitchen. He was standing with his back to her making coffee. Suddenly shy, Rosanna stood in the doorway, waiting for him to notice her. Aware of her presence, he turned his head. Nodding briefly, he rested his eyes on her indifferently for a moment.

'Coffee and rolls?' he asked politely.

'Yes, please.' She sat down, deflated, wondering at his mood, uncertain what to say. And then she noticed that he wasn't in the shorts he had worn each morning. He was dressed formally in silk suit, shirt and tie. Uneasiness and a faint alarm began to show in her eyes as she remained silent. Putting the coffee on to the table, Carlo sat down, and she noticed he hadn't cooked himself anything to eat. Suddenly her appetite deserted her.

'I'm afraid we have to get back today,' he said quietly, spooning sugar into his coffee.

'Business?' she hazarded.

'For heaven's sake, Rosanna, you're not going to start an inquisition every time our plans have to be changed, are you?' he asked irritably.

She didn't answer as her happiness and self-confidence began to slip away. What had she done? she wondered. Could she be wrong about last night? Had it been merely an obligation to him? Had his feelings not been involved as she had thought? Her throat contracted painfully. She felt confused, unsure.

'I'll clear up here,' Carlo said coldly, 'while you get your things together. I'm all packed and I'd like to make an early start.'

'Fine,' she said quietly, not looking at him.

Suddenly the phone shrilled, and Rosanna jumped. She didn't know there was a phone at the villa. Carlo got up to answer it. 'You won't be long, will you?' he asked, turning at the door.

She looked at him, her face controlled, expression-less, her eyes clear and empty. 'I won't be long,' she said firmly.

For a moment they stared at each other, both faces shuttered while the phone continued to ring, and Rosanna fought to keep her face from breaking up with anguish.

At last Carlo nodded and left. A moment later she heard his voice: '*Si, pronto,* Maria. . . .'

And then Rosanna panicked. Like a streak she ran upstairs to her room, closing the door and locking herself in. Calmly she walked to the communicating door and locked that too, the click loud in the silent room. Then she sank on to the bed, her hands to her face, as the pain began. Last night had meant nothing to him: that was what she had to face. He hadn't shared her emotions as she had thought. He had pretended to care, and she wondered dully what else in the last days had been pretence—the laughter, the companionship, everything?

She had no experience of men and had no idea such feelings could be faked. Or perhaps he had desired her, enjoying the novelty of a conquest made against the heavy odds of her ignorance, her nervousness and the hang-ups and inhibitions from her childhood. Possibly she had given him a momentary satisfaction, a minor triumph for an ego bored and satiated with too many eager women.

Shame burst through her feelings and the blood flushed her body as she remembered how much she had given, how completely and easily she had succumbed to his expertise, his technique.

How could she now face going back to Palermo with him, living in his home, trying to build a façade for his family and friends?

'Rosanna?' It was his voice from downstairs. 'Are you ready?'

She unlocked the door and walked to the head of the stairs. He was in the hall below, a suitcase in each hand.

'Carlo,' she asked dully, 'would it be possible for me to stay here?'

He stood still and looked up at her, his face shuttered, his eyes narrowed, hiding his expression.

'No,' he said bluntly. 'Once you're pregnant you'll come back here and stay till the birth of the baby. Now we return together.'

He turned and walked out of the front door.

CHAPTER SIX

THE heat was sweltering, and Rosanna was glad to see an empty table on the terrace of the crowded *pasticceria*. She put down her parcels and subsided with relief into a chair in the cool shade of the umbrella. She ordered an *espresso* and a bottle of iced mineral water, glad of the crowd around her. Somewhere, she knew, Enrico was keeping her in his line of vision. But for the moment she had escaped. Escape!

During those early weeks after their return from Cefalu she had thought of little else. At first she hadn't believed Carlo when he had spelt out the rules of their life together.

'I don't understand,' she had protested, bewildered.

'It's quite simple. You are never at any time or for any reason to leave this house alone.'

'But Carlo, that's impossible!' Her voice was agitated. 'I know no one in Palermo. I have no friends on the island. It would mean I could never go out!'

'That's nonsense. You'll make friends.' His quiet deep voice had the steely inflection she had come to recognise. 'There's my family. I'm sure Maria would bear you company whenever she's free. And if all else fails, you'll have Enrico to take you.'

'You can't mean it!' She had been incredulous. 'It's mad, mediaeval! I'm perfectly safe on the streets of Palermo—like a hundred other women. What could happen to me?'

'You aren't any woman. You're a Vicenzi. What's more, you'll do as I say.' His voice rose arrogantly. 'So far I've indulged your taste for argument, but this is now finished. In future you'll do exactly as I say' he went on icily, 'and stop subjecting me to your opinions on every subject that arises.'

She had ranted, raved, cajoled and tried to reason with him, but he remained adamant, aloof and totally disinterested.

And he'd been clever. He knew exactly how to handle her. Whenever she began to argue or refused to do something he wanted of her, he simply left the room, so that she was forced to trail after him with the servants listening or to stop arguing. One day, in the middle of one of her impassioned pleas, he had actually walked out of the flat. Again and again his arrogance goaded her into speech, even when she knew it was useless to try to reach him.

At the end of three weeks she had been drained, exhausted, and she had stopped. Instead of anger and emotion, she showed Carlo only cool indifference to match his own. She demanded nothing of him, obeyed tacitly his every command and withdrew behind a shell, a wall of defence that he couldn't penetrate. That he didn't choose to try didn't deter her. She knew she would have to become indifferent to him in order to survive. The hatred born that last morning in Cefalu was tearing her apart. It affected Carlo not at all.

And so had been set the pattern of their lives. He left early each morning and Rosanna had no idea where he went, what he did or when he would return. The only time he informed her of his plans was when he wished her to accompany him to visit friends, family or business associates. Then she was told what

to wear and when to be ready. Silently they would
travel, sitting together behind Enrico, not speaking,
sharing nothing, to spend the evening acting out their
supposedly happy marriage, only to return in the same
way, side by side, isolated and apart.

And so had begun the loneliest time of her life. The
house ran like clockwork and she had nothing to do.
When she had suggested to Christina that she would
like to help, to cook a meal occasionally, the older
woman had laughed, grinning hugely at what she
considered an eccentric joke, and returned to her
kitchen shaking her head, perplexed at her mistress.

Rosanna had made one attempt to come to terms
with Maria. She had telephoned, suggesting they had
lunch.

'Why?' Maria had asked sharply.

'I'd like to talk to you, to ask your help,' Rosanna
had improvised.

'Are you pregnant?' Maria had demanded bluntly.

'No.' The older woman must know she couldn't be
aware of any pregnancy so early in her marriage.

'I see.' Maria had been evasive. '*Sì*, Rosanna, we
must have lunch. I'll ring you when I'm free.'

Rosanna hadn't heard from her again. Valli
continued to dress her, and Rosanna no longer
complained or objected to the constant stream of
outfits that continued to arrive from her dress house.

And then, some four weeks after their return to
Palermo, Carlo had come into her bedroom. She woke
to find him undressing by the shaded light of her
bedside lamp.

'What is it?' she had asked, suddenly wide awake.

'What is what?' he had queried lightly.

'What do you want? What are you doing in my
room?' she had become agitated.

'You're my wife,' he had responded amicably. 'If I choose to sleep in your bedroom, I've the right to do so.'

'No . . . No, Carlo, please. . . .' she had panicked. 'I don't want . . . I mean, I'm tired, and it's late.'

'It is late,' he had been unperturbed by her agitation and bent to turn off the light. 'Come, *cara*,' he said as he dropped on to the bed beside her, 'perhaps some of the tension between us can be—er—dispelled.'

And he had made love to her. At first she had fought him, silently and with barely concealed violence, until her resistance crumbled and he broke through her deepest defences. The hatred she had banked down fused into passion, rousing and igniting him beyond anything she had experienced with him in Cefalu, till they collapsed into sleep as dawn crept through the shutters.

After that Carlo slept in her room every night. If they dined at home he would go to his study after dinner and she would hear nothing from him until he followed her to bed, often in the early hours. On the nights he was away from home she would wait for him, seething with fury, resenting his presence in her bed, believing he had come straight from the arms of his sister-in-law. But still she would respond to his lovemaking in a way that often shamed her in the morning.

And he was a superbly skilful lover. He knew every inch of her body and how to rouse her to passionate, ardent response and bring her ecstatic fulfilment. Their inhibitions with each other melted in the weeks that followed as desire between them increased and Rosanna learned how to rouse and satisfy the fiercely passionate needs of his body.

But their life during the day didn't change. Carlo

was always gone when she woke up, and Rosanna marvelled at the twin existence they led—passionate and silent lovers at night, equally silent strangers during the day. Sometimes when they entertained at home she would sense his desire for her. Towards the end of the evening she would find his gaze on her, the hard blue eyes brilliant and intent. And there would be no parting. He would sweep her into his arms and carry her to bed. Then they would make love hungrily again and again, their bodies seemingly insatiable for each other.

But for Rosanna it was never again the joy and happiness of that first night in Cefalu. Then she had given herself without thought or reservation. That had never happened again. However passionately she responded to him, she was aware of an overpowering need to keep from him any knowledge of her deeper feelings.

During those early terrible weeks after their honeymoon, Rosanna had been convinced her only feelings for him were of deep hatred, that her budding tentative love had not survived the battering he had imposed. But, strangely, it hadn't worked out that way. She found herself watching him, learning to read his face.

The pulse at the side of that mobile sensual mouth which could evoke such passionate responses from her body throbbed when he was angry or disturbed. The eyes that could glaze with passion were often hard with boredom or glinting with anger. She noticed that his skin, as dark as ever, was more tautly stretched across the powerful bone structure. And he had thinned in body, as she had herself since their return to Palermo.

Sometimes she would glance at him unexpectedly

across a family dinner table and find his eyes on her, unseeing, bleak and inscrutable. Then her breath would catch with an aching tenderness that she had to control and hide, when she longed to caress his cheek and make him laugh to chase away the shadows in his mind. At times like those she knew her love was just beginning. And she longed to see him again as he had been those few days after their wedding when they had laughed and teased and been together.

And she knew she wasn't well. She had become listless, apathetic, her sparkle dimmed, her eyes totally withdrawn. She tried to fill her days as best she could, shopping with Enrico as her bodyguard, buying things she didn't want or need, filling her days with mindless activities mechanically performed. She had always been a loner, not finding it easy to make friends, and she knew Carlo's friends and relations found her cool and didn't understand her. In turn she made no effort to bridge the gap between them.

And then one night the pattern had changed. As usual she was waiting for the sound of his key in the door. She must have dozed off, and woke sharply as he entered the flat. But he didn't come to bed. Rosanna waited an hour, then another, till she became worried. In bare feet she padded into the hall. There were no lights, and fear suddenly gripped her. Had he brought Maria with him and they were making love in the dark? Was he ill and had collapsed?

She opened the door to the study.

'Don't turn on the light!' Carlo said sharply.

'What is it, Carlo?' she asked anxiously.

'It's nothing,' he said dully. 'Go back to bed.'

As her eyes adjusted to the dark she could see him sitting on the couch, his head in his hands. She knelt down in front of him. He was gripping his scalp with his hands, seeming to grind his head between his fingers, his face pale with pain.

'Your head?' she asked.

'It's nothing, Rosanna—just a headache. Please leave me alone.'

'In a moment.' She stood up. 'Stretch out, face down. Come on!' she commanded.

He sighed, too weary to protest. She waited till he lay full length and then began to massage him—neck, shoulders, the back of the head, slowly, rhythmically, her fingers moving firmly across the knotted muscles, enjoying the feel of the beautifully shaped head. After a while she felt him relax. Her wrists and fingers ached, but still she continued until she heard his deep, even breathing and knew he was asleep. Fetching a rug, she draped it over him and pulled off his shoes. Quietly she turned to leave him, when suddenly he spoke.

'Don't go,' he mumbled.

She stopped, wondering if he was dreaming and thought she was Maria. He reached for her hand and pulled her down beside him.

'Stay with me,' he whispered, and rolled on top of her, his head pillowed against her. A moment later he was asleep.

Rosanna lay cramped and uncomfortable, his head heavy on her breast, his arm flung across her, keeping her by him. And for the first time since Cefalu she felt a glimmer of happiness, a quiet content. Then she, too, slept.

Some time during the night Carlo woke her. She sat up, forgetting where she was. He bent down and picked her up, carrying her to bed. That night he made love with a tenderness and emotion she had not known since their first night together, and she responded with a curious pain, until she fell asleep in his arms.

The next morning she slept late and found Carlo had gone as usual. Still groggy with sleep, she got out of bed. The room began to swim round her and she fell heavily.

She came to on the floor, with Christina's anxious face above her, a blanket wrapped round her.

'Signora!' Christina was chafing her hands. 'Oh, thanks be to God, you are all right! Please do not move. *Il dottore* will be here in a few moments.'

'Oh, no ... it's ... oh dear, you shouldn't have telephoned the doctor, wasting his time.'

Christina was unexpectedly firm. 'It's no waste of time, *signora*,' she said gravely. 'I have been worried— we all are worried. You don't eat, you're pale and thin. It's not good for the child.'

'The child?' Rosanna bit her lip. 'You think I'm pregnant?'

'But *certo* ... of course!' Christina seemed quite sure. 'What else?'

'I can't ... it's too early to say. ...' Rosanna began. 'Please, this is silly. Help me up.'

Christina's face was set, her mouth mutinous. '*Il dottore* said not to move you.'

'I know,' Rosanna said lightly, 'but that was when I was unconscious. Now help me up, Christina, I can't manage alone and I want to get back into bed.'

By the time Dr Albini arrived she was sitting up in bed, washed and refreshed with a hot drink in her hands.

'Good morning,' she smiled brilliantly. 'I'm sorry you've been called for nothing.'

For a moment he looked nonplussed and cast a sharp glance at Christina. What he saw in her face obviously decided him. 'Thank you, Christina, I can manage now,' he said briefly. 'I'll call you if I need you.'

'*Si, signor dottore*,' Christina said quietly, and left.

'Well, young woman, what's all this?' He pulled up a chair and felt for her wrist. 'I'm here, I might as well examine you.'

'On one condition,' Rosanna smiled at him as he looked up in surprise. 'That you don't tell Carlo I fainted.'

'Mm. . . .' he looked into her face rather seriously for a moment. 'I don't pretend to understand you young people. Why shouldn't your husband know if you're not well or with child? He has the right.'

'Of course.' Rosanna looked down at her hands, avoiding his glance. 'But I want to tell him myself.'

'Oh,' his brow cleared, 'that's different. Very well. But you will have to tell him everything. I'll find out soon enough if you haven't done so,' he threatened good humouredly.

The examination was thorough, and his face was grave as he finished and packed away his instruments.

'Well,' he said heavily as he sat down again, 'it does seem that you're with child. It's a little early to be definite, but we should know in a few days.' He picked up her hand and frowned down at it. 'I have to be very angry with you, Rosanna. You know why, don't you?'

She nodded, refusing to meet his eyes.

'You haven't followed my instructions. You're not eating and you're allowing worry and emotion to drain you. You're thin and far from well. It has to stop.'

'Yes,' she whispered, 'I know.'

'So,' he asked urgently, 'what are you going to do about it?'

She shook her head. 'I don't know.'

'You realise you're not going to be fit for motherhood when the time comes?' He paused reflectively. 'I think I'll have to take you into hospital for a while.'

'Oh, no. . . .' Rosanna pleaded, shock in her voice, 'no . . . please, not that!'

'You leave me no choice, my dear. You've shown yourself to be heedless and stubborn, going your own way, refusing to face the facts of your illness. And I'm responsible to Carlo for your health and that of the child.' He paused again, a frown between his eyes. 'I certainly don't want you in hospital—the bed is urgently needed for women who are really ill.' He sighed and stood up. 'I find it difficult to be patient with you.'

'Please,' she whispered, 'will you give me a little time?' she lifted her eyes to his face, and he could see she was close to tears. 'I know what you're saying is fully deserved, but now there's the child, I will do as you ask; everything, exactly,' she promised.

'I don't know if I can trust you, Rosanna.'

'Will you give me two weeks? If I don't follow your instructions, then I will come into hospital for as long as you say. Please let me try,' she pleaded.

He stood uncertain, unwilling to agree. 'Very well,' he said at last, reluctantly, 'but you'll have to check with me regularly?' he insisted.

'I promise,' she said firmly.

And now here she was three days later, most definitely pregnant, on her way to fulfilling her contract, she thought ruefully as she sipped her coffee. Christina had a diet chart and prepared small amounts of tempting dishes four times a day, and these were eaten dutifully.

She knew Doctor Albini was right. She had allowed herself to go to pieces, and it had to stop. She didn't want this child, she told herself, but she did have a duty towards it, and she'd make sure the child didn't suffer at her hands.

The coming months would be the only thing she would have of the baby she and Carlo had made together—the boy, or girl of course. She wondered what Carlo would feel if it was a girl. Her mind shied away from her husband. He would marry Maria and they would bring up her baby . . . together. Pain shot through her at the thought and she closed her mind firmly against stupid and idle speculations about the future. She refused to become morbid or succumb to self-pity.

'But how delightful . . . the beautiful Signora Rosanna Vicenzi!' The voice intruded into her thoughts, and she looked up into a vaguely familiar face, but couldn't place the young man who stood bowing before her. 'You don't remember me—I am desolated! Antonio Manzini, Maria's brother,' he reminded her.

'Of course,' Rosanna smiled politely. 'How are you?'

'Hot,' he answered. 'You permit?' he asked, and sat down. 'I knew this would be my lucky day. And you see I was right.' Dressed in white from his silk shirt and linen suit to impeccable leather moccasins, he looked as though he'd stepped right out of a fashion magazine. Flicking his fingers for the waiter, he ordered iced drinks for them both.

'But you,' he leaned across the table towards her, 'you've changed. Yes,' he speculated, 'when we met at that sad dinner party, you were nervous, shy, a young girl, beautiful of course, but like a doe, apprehensive. And now you're a woman, the innocence has gone

from your eyes. And now of course I shall find you
irresistible.'

Rosanna smiled distantly at his conceit.

'You're not impressed?' he asked after a moment's
silence. The waiter brought drinks and she could feel
Antonio's eyes on her averted head. His humour and
banter didn't appeal to her today.

'You must know how beautiful and desirable you
are,' he went on. 'And surely by this time you have a
lover. Let me see, you've been married . . . two . . .
three months? It's certainly time to take a lover. Your
husband will expect it. And who better than a member
of the family? It makes for discretion. And after all,
Carlo hasn't been slow to return to his former lifestyle.
He and my sister are again . . . so,' he lifted two
fingers and crossed them, 'very close. And of course
with Carlo there are others.' He sighed extravagantly.
'I envy him . . . we all do. How does he do it, we ask
ourselves, the energy. . . .'

He stopped and looked penetratingly into her face,
noting the flush rise from her throat. 'But I see, *cara*,
you're not amused. I'm perhaps not in favour today?'
He paused expectantly, waiting for her to say
something. But she merely smiled again absently.

'Perhaps you don't believe me?' he asked. He leaned
back in his chair, twirling the stem of his glass
between lazy fingers, watching her closely.

'You appear to have lost your so charming sense of
humour. Can it be that you've fallen in love with your
husband? Surely not. In Palermo society that would
be considered a disaster, and in very bad taste.
Husbands are for paying bills and fathering babies,
not for love.'

At last Rosanna was stung into speech. 'I'm so
sorry,' she said coolly. 'I'm afraid I missed what you

said. I've been looking out for Enrico and I see he's arrived. Please excuse me—I must go.' She rose and picked up her parcels.

Antonio jumped to his feet and took them from her, dropping some notes on the table. 'Please, Rosanna, allow me,' and his voice was suddenly serious and strangely gentle. 'I will take you to your car.' And he took her elbow. 'You have courage, *cara*, and this I admire. I think I have been very bad-mannered and I owe you an apology. I hope I'm forgiven.'

'Of course, Antonio,' she replied evenly, 'as you said, it's all family.'

They stepped off the terrace, and Rosanna suddeny faltered and stopped. Immediately ahead of them, at a table for two, Carlo and Maria were sitting, deeply engrossed in each other. Maria had her hand on his arm, and he was leaning forward across the table towards her.

Just then Carlo looked up and saw them, and his face lost its smile, setting hard, blue eyes grim with anger.

Looking away from him, Rosanna suprised an expression of malevolent triumph on Maria's face, quickly masked as she saw her brother.

The moment of tension lasted only seconds, while all four people remained motionless. Rosanna was the first to pull herself together. Walking on slowly, she lifted one hand in a casual salute, smiling as she moved towards the waiting car.

Relinquishing her parcels to Enrico, Antonio took her hand in his and looked into her face. 'Not only courage, my dear,' he said quietly, 'but style. I congratulate you. As I believe I said once before, I envy Carlo his good fortune.' He bent his head and lightly touched his lips to her hand. She nodded her goodbye, smiling briefly as the car moved and he was lost from view.

Rosanna's neck felt rigid with the effort at self-control. Seeing Carlo with Maria had jolted her more than any of the malicious things Antonio had said. Jealousy gripped her as she imagined them together and how they would spend the rest of the afternoon. Sudden nausea rose in her throat and she fought for composure. She would have to get used to hearing of her husband's love life outside his marriage, just as she had to accept his feelings for Maria. She wondered what would happen once he knew she was pregnant. His part of the contract would then be finished. Would it mean their life together would end?

Christina opened the front door before the lift had stopped and Rosanna walked into the hall, Enrico behind her with her parcels.

'What is it?' she asked, looking into the anxious face of the older woman.

'You have a visitor,' Christina whispered.

'Who is it?'

'Signora Vicenzi,' Christina announced. '*La mamma del* Signor Conte.'

CHAPTER SEVEN

ROSANNA walked slowly over to the hall mirror and took off her hat. Smoothing her hair nervously with fingers that trembled slightly, she met Christina's eyes in the glass.

'How long has the *signora* been here?' she asked.

'Only a little while. She asked me to ring Signor Carlo, but he wasn't in his office. I left a message.'

No, thought Rosanna cynically, he's too busy with personal matters to be in his office.

'Thank you,' she said now, 'I'll see the *signora*. Please bring refreshments.'

'*Si, signora*, it is in preparation,' Christina replied, and walked off to the kitchen.

Rosanna looked at her own reflection in the mirror and wished Carlo had told her about his mother. Did he know she was coming? Would she stay with them? Uneasily she wondered why Carlo's mother had come to Palermo now. Dismissing her silly premonitions, she walked across the hall into the living room.

Standing by the window, smoking a cigarette, was a tall, slim elegant woman, and for a moment she didn't hear Rosanna. From the door Rosanna saw sleek blonde hair expertly coiffeured, a printed silk suit impeccably tailored to a beautiful figure, long slender legs in sheer silk and feet shod in softest kid high-heeled sandals. Carlo's mother?

'Signora Vicenzi?' Rosanna's voice was quiet in the silent room. The woman at the window turned, and Rosanna looked into the deep blue of her husband's eyes. 'I'm Rosanna, Carlo's wife,' she said in Italian.

'Oh, please, honey, don't let's talk in Italian—so exhausting!'

Rosanna gasped audibly. That slow drawl was unmistakable. Carlo's mother was American!

They were interrupted by Christina's arrival with one of the maids carrying a tray which was put on to the low coffee table.

'Thank you,' Rosanna nodded to Christina, 'I'll manage now.'

'Ah, at last!' Signora Vicenzi walked over to the tray, helping herself liberally to whisky from the decanter. Ignoring ice and soda, she drank it thirstily before she refilled her glass and sat down. 'I must tell you right away, honey, this has been a great shock to me,' she began. 'I've been away visitng friends in South America for the last three months and knew nothing about Carlo's marriage.'

She paused for a moment to drink again, and Rosanna offered some of the delicious *panettoni*, the Sicilian currant bread that Christina baked.

'No.' Carlo's mother put out her hand as if to ward off the food. 'I never—but never—touch anything sweet. More than my life's worth! I fight all the time against weight.'

Rosanna smiled. 'Very successfully.' She looked across at her mother-in-law, searching for points of resemblance with her son. In repose she looked older than she had seemed across the room, tiny networks of lines visible through the heavy make-up, the flesh stretched thinly across the bones, giving a sharpness to the face, the neck unexpectedly scrawny, revealing the dieting to which the body was subjected.

'Gee, where was I?' her mother-in-law continued. 'Oh, yes. When I got back I found the letter—not from Carlo, you understand, he didn't bother to let me know, but from Canada—from my daughter Luisa.'

Luisa. So Carlo had a sister he had never mentioned.

'I must tell you, honey, that never in a million years would I have expected Carlo to marry a foreigner. Never!'

'I'm half Sicilian,' Rosanna murmured.

'Well, all I can say is I hope you can handle him.' She looked across at Rosanna. 'How old are you?'

'Twenty.'

'Well, I don't envy you what you've taken on, and I sure hope you've some experience of men.' She sighed and lit another cigarette, looking at Rosanna across the flame. 'I bet he didn't mention my existence to you,' she said suddenly. 'I guess I'm as much of a shock to you as your marriage was to me.' She leaned forward. 'Tell me, did he fall in love with you? Or did you bring him some business connection like Giovanna?'

Rosanna opened her mouth to make a placating reply but was forestalled.

'Oh, what the hell . . . you probably don't know that any more than I. He's so devious and secretive, and I bet that hasn't changed.'

Rosanna felt she had to stop this slandering of her husband. 'I'm sorry that Carlo isn't here to meet you,' she said quietly.

'Don't let that worry you, honey. I didn't know myself till the last moment—I never plan. Mind, Luisa was dead against my coming. Carlo wouldn't want it, she said on the phone, wants you to himself for a while. But in the end I had to come anyway— some business he has to attend to for me. I hope it won't take long' Signora Vicenzi shuddered. 'I'd forgotten how much I dislike Sicily.'

'I can understand that,' Rosanna murmured. 'Unhappy memories. . . .'

'Sure, there's that . . . but I never liked Sicily. Carlo's father and I married in the States. Did he tell you? No, I guess not. Carlo never does talk of his family. . . .'

She leaned back, her glass in her hand. 'Gino was in the States on business and he swept me right off my feet. I'd never met anyone like him,' she reminisced. 'I was just seventeen and he was dark, kind of brooding . . . irresistible—all that virility . . . ugh! I fell real hard.' She laughed lightly. 'My father was dead against it—*Mafioso*, he called Gino. But Gino was a count, and that swung it for my mother. And all that money! My mother loved money and she felt Gino could keep me in the style to which I was accustomed.'

She paused to lean forward and refill her glass. 'But as soon as Gino got me here everything changed. All he could think about was having children. I was eighteen when Luisa was born, but that wasn't enough for Gino. Sicilian males think about sons before they're out of short pants, and Gino was no exception. When the twins were born I was just twenty, and I told Gino no more. He agreed and we began to lead separate lives. Or—to be exact—he led his life, where women came and went like new suits, while I was confined to the villa and the awful—truly awful Vicenzi family.'

Watching his mother drink deeply, Rosanna wondered what Carlo felt about her. Why had he failed to let her know about his marriage when the rest of the family had been told?

'I begged Gino to let me go home,' Signora Vicenzi went on, her voice slightly blurred, 'but he was adamant. When the children were grown up, he said, he would reconsider. But he never did, of course. So I wrote to my father. But he was suddenly obstinate. My place was with my husband, he wrote; I had to learn to understand him and accept the life I'd chosen.' She gestured with her hands, the rings on her fingers sparkling. 'So I stayed. And then of course I adored Luigi. We were very close . . . always. Wicked, he was,' she said gleefully, 'truly wicked. Very like his father who spoilt him rotten and adored him. Did you know he was blond like me?' She turned to look at Rosanna for a moment, then leaned back, her eyes and mind on the past. 'Luigi took after me in everything. I've some pictures somewhere.' She coughed lightly. 'You'd have adored him,' she went on. 'All the girls did . . . went wild about him. . . .'

She stopped again, flicking the diamond-studded lighter to begin another cigarette, the last, half finished, ground into the ashtray. 'Carlo adored his brother too, followed him around like a pet lamb. Luigi used to get impatient, tell him to live his own life. You know what boys are.'

Rosanna interrupted. 'Have you any pictures of Carlo as a little boy?' she asked eagerly.

'Oh, sure, there must be some. The boys were always being taken together. But Carlo was sullen, like his father—looked like him too . . . and so terribly glum, serious. He still is—no fun, no laughter in him.'

She sat back, resting her head against the cushions, her eyes closed, cigarette in one hand, glass in the other. Suddenly her jaw clenched and she opened her eyes wide, looking over Rosanna's head. 'And then they got Luigi,' she said tightly. 'And, we were so careful—bodyguards, dogs, bullet-proof cars, the lot. But they got him, and it was meant for Carlo. Carlo was the younger twin, but the brains of the business.

And it was all the fault of that stupid girl, Giovanna— Carlo's wife. They saw her and thought it was Carlo behind the wheel of the car. But she'd fallen for Luigi like everyone else, and it was Luigi she was with that day.' She laughed mirthlessly. 'She thought he loved her—gee, that was funny! He and I used to have some laughs about that. To him she was just another body.'

Her face twisted with sudden pain. 'I can see it all so clearly,' she whispered, 'how he would have tried to get rid of her, and she would have pleaded with him to take her. And in the end he did. And it cost him his life.'

She put her hand to her head in sudden weariness. 'It should have been Carlo at the end of that bullet,' she murmured. 'Only it wasn't. And we all died. Luigi died instantly, Giovanna later that night, and my husband died of grief two years later, bitter and twisted, blaming Carlo for his brother's death. And I died too . . . a little. The day after the funeral I left Sicily.'

When she finally stopped talking the silence in the room vibrated with tension. Rosanna felt faint with revulsion at what she'd heard. She had to get out of the room, away from this woman to whom she owed respect and affection.

'Excuse me, please . . . for a moment,' she began, but her mother-in-law didn't hear her, lost in her memories. Nor did she notice as Rosanna rose unsteadily and turned to go, halting in sudden shock.

Carlo was standing in the doorway, motionless, his face pale, his eyes bleak and empty as he looked at her.

How long had he been standing there? How much had he heard? she wondered, an aching pity stirring in her. Instinctively she moved towards him, wanting only to touch him, to erase that terrible look from his eyes. But before she could reach him, his mother had seen him.

'Carlo darling!' she swept past Rosanna and reached up to embrace her son. 'We were just getting acquainted, and I was telling—er—her about . . . old times. . . .' her voice tailed off.

'Hello, Mamma,' Carlo said quietly. 'I wasn't expecting you.' He stood quite still, his arms at his side, as his mother reached up to kiss him.

Rosanna murmured something inaudible and fled. Upstairs she sat on the bed, unable to think coherently. Pictures kept flashing through her mind of Carlo as a handsome little boy, measuring himself against the brother he adored, desperate to win the love of his parents who couldn't see him beside the brother they idolised.

And a mother who could wish him dead instead of his brother! How was it possible for any mother to think such monstrous, terrible things? Was this the reason for the loneliness she sensed in him? For his love for Maria? They'd shared so much horror and pain, perhaps it was natural they should turn to each other for the love denied them in their marriages.

She didn't know how long she sat, deep in her own thoughts, heedless of the time or her guest below.

Suddenly the door opened and Carlo came in quietly, closing it behind him. He looked at her pale, set face, the twisted handkerchief between her fingers, and walked over to the open window.

'I came to tell you that Mamma has decided not to stay with us,' he said tonelessly. 'She'll stop with Maria. I'm taking her over there now and may stay on . . . possibly overnight. Don't expect me back.'

He turned to face her. She hadn't moved, but she looked up at him. 'Very well, Carlo, if that's what she wants. I'll come down and say my goodbyes.'

'That's not necessary,' he said quickly. 'I'll make

your apologies. You may see her again before she leaves ... possibly,' he ended grimly. 'I'll see you tonight, Rosanna, or tomorrow.'

She didn't answer and he stopped in the doorway. 'Are you all right?' he asked sharply.

'Yes, quite all right, thank you,' she mumbled.

'Mm ... he seemed reluctant to go. 'I'll leave you, then.'

'Goodbye, Carlo,' she said quietly.

Rosanna lay by the pool. The wind was cool against her arms and the late afternoon sun shone weakly through the clouds. The air held the breath of autumn. Soon it would be winter and the endless summer skies would be gone.

Carlo hadn't returned the night his mother arrived and Rosanna had twisted and tossed in bed, jealousy creating havoc in her imagination—pictures of Carlo and Maria floating in and out of her mind. She hadn't slept, and as soon as she heard early morning movements in the kitchen she had rung for Christina.

Quietly she had explained what she wanted. The villa in Cefalu was to be opened up ready for her to move into that afternoon, and Enrico was to be prepared to leave later in the morning.

'But, *signora*,' Christina was clearly worried, '*il signore*—does he know?'

'Please do as I ask,' Rosanna replied coldly. 'Naturally I will leave a note for my husband.'

Christina had recognised a new note of authority in her mistress's voice and had gone to make the arrangements.

Arrived at the villa, Rosanna had been restless hoping constantly to hear from her husband, but he hadn't contacted her. No doubt he was relieved she had gone and guessed the reason. She wondered if he had continued to stay with Maria. She only knew she missed him. The nights especially were hard. She was lonely for him, wanting him to share her bed, the physical intimacy better than no contact at all.

And she wondered what was now in store for her. Would Carlo turn his back on her as lightly as he had taken her, his deepest feelings untouched? Whatever was in store for her, there was little point in brooding. Her wishes wouldn't be consulted, and she had to accept the situation and come to terms with it, living from day to day to get through the months ahead till the baby was born.

And certainly she had plenty of life round her to help. At the crack of dawn Signora Carvallo arrived with one or other of her many daughters and the women took over the villa, bringing the house alive with talk and laughter. While they scrubbed and polished, they would talk volubly to each other, shouting if need be from different rooms. Silence overtook them only at mealtimes, when they sat in the kitchen eating their way through the *signora*'s huge plates of pasta.

In her forties, the *signora* was large with curly black hair crowning a round face, eyes sparkling to match the huge gilt rings swinging in her ears. She ruled her family with a rod of iron.

In the mornings her husband drove up in their little van piled high with children in the front and vegetables for their shop in the back. Those members of the family spending the day at the villa tumbled out, and the *signora* would then issue a spate of instructions to the rest.

Her husband, a thin, small, dark-haired man with a brown creased face, would smile and nod, putting in the odd word. '*Si, mamma, si, certo....*' before he turned the van and drove off, still pursued by his wife's voice as she stood in the driveway waving and shouting until he disappeared.

In the evenings Papa returned to collect the women, and their voices would be raised in quarrelsome and happy laughter, echoing down the drive and rising above the spluttering of the van's ancient engine.

At first the *signora* had tried to persuade Rosanna to share their midday meal. 'It is good for the *bambino*,' she had insisted graphically, pointing to her own rounded stomach and shouting slightly as though Rosanna, being English, was bound to be a little deaf and perhaps not altogether right in the head.

The next day a huge iron pot emerged from beneath the vegetables in the van and Rosanna was invited into the kitchen to taste the *signora*'s *osso bucco*, the famous Italian spicy dish of veal, tomatoes and rice which the *signora* had specially prepared to tempt Rosanna's appetite. Feeling more than a little guilty, Rosanna explained in faultless Italian why she was unable to eat it, but the *signora* was not convinced.

'To make strong sons,' she insisted, 'it's necessary to eat two good meals a day—and always pasta.' The bits she prepared for Rosanna from the diet sheet she didn't consider suitable or adequate for a mother-to-be.

Rosanna shivered. It was time to go in. Walking up the garden deep in thought, she didn't see she was being watched. Looking up suddenly, she saw Christina coming down the steps towards her.

Rosanna stopped in sudden fear. 'Signor Carlo!' she whispered. 'Something has happened?'

'No, no, *signora*, nothing.' Christina reassured her quickly, taking Rosanna's beach bag. 'The Signor

Conte has sent me to look after you.'

'No,' Rosanna's voice was firm. 'I've the Carvallos. I want you to go back to Palermo, to look after my husband.'

'My cousin, she is at the flat and she's a good girl. She cooks, cleans and keeps all in order. In any case the *signore* is hardly there. No, I stay to see to you and the *bambino*.'

Rosanna looked anxiously at the other woman. 'You didn't tell him about the baby, did you, Christina?'

'Certainly not, you know me better than that, *signora*,' she answered proudly.

Rosanna was contrite. 'I'm sorry, I shouldn't have asked.'

'No, *signora*, you shouldn't,' the older woman said with dignity. 'And now it's time to go in. You need a hot bath and a meal. I shall not of course complain, but it is good I am here to look after you—properly,' she stressed.

Later that evening when she had sent a tired Christina to bed, Rosanna sat downstairs in the dark, her eyes on the black expanse of sea, the brooding cloudy sky above.

The scene matched her thoughts, she mused dryly. She had no wish to think about her husband, his return to his former life before his marriage, and she felt restless, dreading the empty bedroom and another sleepless night.

Opening the glass doors, she stepped out on to the terrace, the wind tangling her hair, cold against her face.

Suddenly she stood still. The flash of headlights travelled briefly across the terrace and she heard a car pull up beyond the wall separating her from the forecourt of the villa.

Who could it be so late at night? Vaguely frightened, she wondered if she should wake Christina. They were isolated here, away from the town, set back from the main road.

A car door banged and a firm tread sounded on the steps. Her hand stole to her throat. She knew that step. In the dark silence she heard the key in the lock. The light went on in the hall and someone ran swiftly upstairs.

Above her the light came on in her bedroom, and she was now certain who it was. Then she heard Carlo's voice.

'Christina, where are you. The *signora* is not in her room.'

She heard Christina's reply. Doors banged as they searched and then both came downstairs. At last Rosanna moved. She crossed the living room and stepped out into the hall just as Carlo reached for the telephone.

'I'm here,' she said, and her voice sounded unnaturally quiet and rather hoarse. 'I was out on the terrace.'

Dressed formally in a blue silk suit, tall and broad-shouldered, Carlo looked so familiar, her throat contracted with sudden emotion. His hair was untidy as though he'd just run his hand through it, and he looked deathly tired, black shadows round his eyes which now gazed at her, strangely intent, taking in the bare legs, the short dress and the loose, windswept hair.

Rosanna heard him expel his breath as he put down the receiver.

'I'm sorry, Christina,' she said softly, 'please go back to bed.'

The older woman was standing half way up the stairs pale with shock, staring at them both. '*Si, signora*' she said quietly, '*buona notte.*'

Rosanna turned and walked into the living room, turning on lights as she went. Her heart was hammering, her throat dry, and she kept her back to her husband so that he wouldn't see her face and guess how she longed to throw herself into his arms.

'Would you like something to eat?' she asked evenly.

'No,' he replied, the soft voice suddenly harsh. He walked past her to the window and she sensed anger in him, repressed and only just under control.

'I hope there's nothing ... wrong?' she asked nervously. 'Everyone's well?'

'No, nothing's wrong,' he replied heavily. 'I've just driven here from the airport. My mother left for Miami this evening.'

Rosanna sat down.

'I've spent the last days at her side,' he went on wearily. 'She had some problems that needed attention.'

'I see. Can I get you a drink, Carlo, some coffee?'

'I'll help myself.' He turned to the drinks table and poured himself a brandy, splashing soda into it. She waited, tense now, for him to tell her why he had come.

'Rosanna,' he asked quietly, 'what did my mother tell you to make you run away?'

'Run away?' she echoed, bewildered.

'The day my mother arrived ... in the bedroom. You looked ...' he breathed deeply, 'shaken, pale ... possibly angry. I don't know. I couldn't stop to find out. I had to go back to her. As I left you said goodbye, and when I came back the next day you'd gone.'

'But you had my note . . .?'

'Yes, of course.' He was getting impatient. 'I wouldn't be here otherwise and I wouldn't have sent Christina. I want to know why you left suddenly without waiting till I got back. Christina said she thought you were upset.'

'I'm sorry you discuss me with the servants!' Rosanna said angrily.

'For heaven's sake, Rosanna, Christina isn't a servant! Please, don't let's quarrel. I'm not up to it tonight.'

She didn't say anything.

'Well, are you going to tell me?' he asked jerkily.

'Why I came down here?' She paused a moment. 'Yes, I'll tell you. But you should know, because it was you told me to come here. Only you seem to have forgotten.'

He walked up to her, his glass in his hand, his eyes on her face. Nervous at his nearness, she brushed past him to stand with her back to him. In this angry mood he was unpredictable, and she was afraid.

'Well, Rosanna, is it so difficult?' he asked harshly, his voice breaking slightly as though his control was slipping. 'If you couldn't put it in your note, and you've been talking in riddles in the last few minutes, perhaps you can now tell me in words I can understand.'

She shivered apprehensively. 'Very well.' She turned to face him, her head up, her eyes on his face. 'I'm pregnant,' she said flatly.

Carlo stiffened abruptly and suddenly the glass in his hand shattered on to the carpet, a thin trickle of blood oozing from one finger. He took no notice of the broken glass or his bleeding hand. In one stride he was in front of her, his hands on her bare arms, as he began to shake her, his face wild with fury, eyes blazing with anger out of control.

'You lying, cheating bitch!' he snarled. 'And who's the father? Do you know who it is? Is it Antonio Manzini . . . is it?'

'No, Carlo, no . . . of course not.' Her voice weakened and she felt faint with fear as he continued to shake her. Her head began to swim and she felt herself fall, limp in his arms. He groaned sharply and picked her up in his arms, dropping her ungently down on to the sofa.

Crunching the broken glass under his shoes, he walked over to the drinks table and poured another brandy.

Rosanna was gulping in air, breathing unevenly, trying to compose herself, to understand what he had said.

She took the glass from him and drank down the spirit, waiting till it cleared her head.

Carlo was standing at the window his back to her, and the room was unnaturally quiet as she waited for him to explain.

'I . . . can't . . . I'm not able to . . . have children,' he said heavily at last.

She looked up in blank astonishment. 'No,' she whispered, 'that's impossible! If it was true I couldn't be pregnant.'

He didn't say anything, and a new thought struck her. 'But, Carlo, the contract . . . if you believe that why did you agree—my grandfather . . .?' Her voice tailed away.

Her question seemed to hover in the silence of the room. He still stood motionless as though he hadn't heard her. Then he began to speak, his voice empty of all feeling, expressionless.

'My first marriage was arranged by my parents . . .

my brother Luigi and I were to marry two sisters.' He hesitated. 'Before the contract was signed Luigi and I had to undergo tests to see if ... we could have children. Luigi's test was positive, mine was negative. I couldn't have children.

'In spite of this the marriages went ahead. I was too young to be interested in having a family, and Giovanna, my wife . . . was quite pleased also.' He paused. 'Some years passed and I began to wonder about those tests. Why did Luigi and Maria not have children? Why had my father-in-law permitted the marriages to go ahead in spite of my test? Luigi and I discussed the possibility that the girls couldn't have children and the tests had been falsified to throw the blame on us. But we weren't sure, and neither of us were particularly interested.'

He walked over to the drinks cabinet and poured himself another brandy. He lifted the glass and then put it down again. Suddenly he looked at her across the room.

'Then my brother ... died,' he said harshly, the pain raw in his eyes and voice, 'and so did my wife.' He turned away. 'When your grandfather's contract came up I ... I was older ... I don't know—perhaps I hoped the tests had been falsified, and there were other reasons—strong reasons for me to accept and hope. . . .'

Rosanna sat stunned, unable to take it in. None of it made sense. Maria had told her on that very first day that she couldn't have children, that this was the reason why Carlo had agreed to her grandfather's marriage contract. How did that fit in with what Carlo had just told her?

She looked across at her husband. He was standing tense and rigid, hands clenched. She sensed how important this was to him and wondered how she could convince him.

Suddenly he whirled round to face her, his mouth set, his eyes probing hers, dark, and intent.

'Well, Rosanna,' he asked huskily, 'were they wrong?'

Slowly she stood up and walked towards him, standing close to the tensely controlled body, looking up into his strained face, her own eyes clear and untroubled.

'Yes,' she said firmly, 'they were wrong. The child I'm bearing is yours, Carlo, and could be no one else's. I can't offer you any proof—but you'll know it when the time comes and you see your likeness in him.' She smiled, her eyes misty, her lips curved into gentle amusement. 'It's a funny old world, isn't it?' she murmured, 'it seems after all I'm not frigid and you're not barren.'

She watched, fascinated, as his face relaxed at her words, his brow cleared. The eyes softened and he lifted one finger to her cheek, stroking it softly.

'No, little one,' he murmured, 'you're not frigid, are you?' and his mouth curled into a gentle smile.

For a moment they looked at each other, their guards down, emotion throbbing between them, and Rosanna prayed for him to take her into his arms and show her the love and tenderness she craved. Breathlessly she waited.

Then he seemed to withdraw, the eyes cooled. 'When is it to be?' he asked, and the moment passed.

She dropped her eyes. 'Shortly before Easter.'

'And what does Albini say?'

'He . . . I . . . have to. . . .'

'I want the truth, Rosanna,' he demanded tautly.

'I don't lie,' she said proudly.

'So?'

She took a deep breath. 'I have to be careful. If I don't . . . eat properly and sleep and rest, he'll take me into hospital . . . to stay. And he knows how much I'd dislike that.'

'That brings me back to my first question, then,' he said. 'What made you run away from Palermo and come down here?'

'I didn't run away. I came down here because you said . . . that last morning here. . . .' she blushed and faltered. 'I asked you if I could stay and you said I'd be coming back to stay when I was pregnant. Don't you remember?'

For a moment he looked down into her eyes rather blindly and she wondered what she had said to make him withdraw from her again. Then he turned away.

'And do you think,' he asked heavily, 'here you'll be able to eat, rest and sleep?'

Rosanna felt the pain at his question. It was what she'd feared—he didn't want her in Palermo. Well, she certainly wouldn't force herself on him or intrude where she wasn't wanted.

'Do you?' Carlo insisted with a strange urgency.

'Yes'.

There was such a long silence that Rosanna wondered if he'd heard her.

'Very well,' he said at last, his voice studied and cool, 'I'll make all the necessary arrangements.'

'If by arrangements you mean Enrico staying here with me, that's not necessary. Nothing can happen to me here.'

'I'm fully aware of how much your freedom means to you, Rosanna,' he said coldly, 'and you should be happy that you'll be returning to it. But while you're in Sicily you're under my protection and I will decide what's necessary. It's even more important now there's the child to consider.'

He sighed wearily. 'I would have thought you'd understand a little better now that you know ... my mother told you ... how my brother died. ...'

Rosanna went white at his words and turned away from him. The moment of affection and understanding between them had gone. His concern was now for the baby, her welfare was only important because she was the mother.

'Very well, Carlo,' she said stiffly, fearful she would break down and beg him to take her with him. 'If that's all, I think I'll go to bed. It's late.'

'Certainly,' he said harshly, 'you need have no fears I'll disturb you. I'll bed down in the dressing room for a few hours. I have to be away early in the morning.'

She stopped in the doorway. 'Carlo,' she asked, suddenly wistful, wishing he would turn round so that she could see his face, 'are you ... do you believe me ... that the baby's yours?'

For a long moment he didn't answer. Then he spoke softly, his voice controlled, the drawl pronounced. 'It's as you say, Rosanna, we'll wait till the child is born. Then we'll know.'

The pain stabbed through her at his words, and she looked at his tall back hoping he would relent. But he didn't move, and she walked out of the room and upstairs, to lie in her bed dry-eyed for the rest of the night.

As the sun came hazily through the shutters she heard him move. Half an hour later his car started up and she listened till the last lingering sound of the engine died away. Then she turned her face to the pillow and wept.

CHAPTER EIGHT

IT was raining. Rosanna watched the windscreen wipers moving rhythmically as the rain spat and hissed against the glass. The straight expanse of motorway stretched as far as the eye could see, and the wind sighed through the palm trees, bending them gracefully towards the road. The world seemed empty as the car sped effortlessly towards Palermo.

Christmas had come and gone, and Rosanna had been alone so long she wondered if she would ever again be able to live among people. She had seen nothing of her husband, and depression had settled deeply into her mind. She lived from day to day, hoping for nothing, without joy at the prospect of the coming child.

Physically she was in better health than she had been for years. The outdoor life she led even when the weather was cold, together with the cossetting she received from Christina, had brought a new softness to her features, a roundness to her body and a glow to her skin. Only the pain at the back of her eyes and the unnatural gravity of her face gave any indication that she wasn't perfectly content.

She had no right or reason to complain. She lived a life many young women would envy. There had been nothing in her contract about the care she would receive during pregnancy, and she had Carlo to thank for the luxury he provided so generously. Even Marco, her bodyguard and constant companion, had turned out to be young, cheerful and engaging.

That Carlo had no wish for her company while the baby was growing inside her was hardly his fault. That she seemed unable to stop loving him and missing him was her problem.

She had been surprised that morning when Christina anounced who it was wishing to see her.

'*Signora!*' Enrico had bowed and smiled, his eyes involuntarily dropping to the signs of the coming baby. 'You are well?'

'Thank you.' She had nodded, waiting for an explanation.

'I've come to take you to Palermo, *signora*.'

'Marco?' she had queried.

'Will spend a little time with his family—a holiday,' Enrico had explained.

'You're taking me to the hospital and back?'

'No, *signora*, not today. The Signor Conte wishes me to drive you home.'

She looked at him wide-eyed and apprehensive, her feelings in unaccustomed turmoil. She didn't want to see Carlo. Nor did she want him to see her as she was, large with child. The last time they had met she had been slim with the figure he desired. She dreaded seeing aversion in his face, possibly disgust. And she wasn't sure if she could cope with the pain and the longing of being with him. Her emotions weren't as tightly under control as they had been.

The flat looked exactly the same—darker after the glass and modernity of Cefalu, but familiar as a home should be. There were no fresh flowers and the place seemed almost too tidy, as though no one really lived there. Cynically she reflected this was probably so. No doubt Carlo was living elsewhere by this time.

She wandered into the living room and stopped

suddenly in the doorway. A woman was sitting on the sofa, her back to Rosanna, a tray with coffee and biscuits on the low table in front of her.

'Hello, Rosanna. I've been waiting to see you.' It was Maria.

Rosanna walked up to her and looked down into that flawless face with its impeccable make-up. She was dressed in her favourite black, diamonds flashing in her ears and on those soft hands.

'Hello, Maria,' Rosanna said politely, 'how are you?'

The other woman looked her over from top to toe and shuddered.

'Thank goodness I can't have children! I could never go through with it, looking as you do for months on end.'

Rosanna's mouth tightened in dislike as she sat down, putting out her hands to the warmth of the crackling log fire. What was Maria doing here? Had she moved in with Carlo? Were they living openly together? Unlikely, she thought. Carlo wouldn't install his mistress in the home of his wife.

It was all becoming too difficult. Her head ached and she hadn't the strength to cross swords with her sister-in-law.

A discreet knock brought a diversion. It was Christina.

'Lunch is ready in your room, *signora*. It is time for your rest.' She drew up a small table to Rosanna's elbow and put down a glass of hot tea, and for once Rosanna didn't object to her fussing. 'Don't be long,' she chided before she left.

'I see you've converted Christina,' Maria said tight-lipped. 'Perhaps it'll be better to replace her when you go. I can't have her caring for the child if she's forever going to talk to him about you.'

A shaft of pain hit Rosanna at her words. Closing her mind to her own future without Carlo and the baby was one thing, having it spelt out by Carlo's future wife was another.

'You said you were waiting for me,' she said coldly. 'What can I do for you?'

'I want to talk to you,' Maria said bluntly. 'I'm very displeased with you, Rosanna. The last time we talked I warned you things would be difficult if you and I didn't come to some arrangement.'

'Difficult for you or for me?' Rosanna asked lightly.

'Don't be insolent!' Maria was going red in the face with anger. 'I warned you about Carlo, but you wouldn't listen. You thought you could have everything your own way. Well, you can't!'

Rosanna watched as she seemed to be releasing some emotion held too long in check.

'Carlo knows you've fallen in love with him,' she went on dramatically. 'He should know the signs—all his women fall for him. It's funny really—as soon as they fall in love with him he gets bored. That's one reason he loves me. I don't throw myself at him all the time. Nor do I make scenes over his little affairs. They're not important ... and I understand his ... needs.' She leaned forward towards Rosanna, suddenly agitated. 'I suppose you've discovered he's a marvellous lover. Well, it means nothing. It's just a routine, an outlet ... it's me he loves and only me. . . .' Her voice rose, hysterical, the smooth flawless face suddenly contorted into ugliness.

Rosanna sat quite still. Carlo knew she loved him? Could that be true? Was that why he hadn't wanted her in Palermo all these months? She should have known. Just as he was expert in his lovemaking, so he would be equally skilful in recognising a woman's emotions. How could she ever have thought to fool him? And Maria was right: he would be bored with her as soon as he guessed the truth about her feelings.

'Well?' Maria was regaining control over herself. 'What do you say to that? Perhaps your pride is a little humbled now. All that success you enjoyed so much last year, deceiving our family and friends, pretending Carlo loved you. I longed to tell them the truth and turn their envy of him into the contempt you deserved—but I wouldn't humiliate him.' She breathed deeply, hatred steaming from her tight face and taut little body.

'So, Maria, what is it you want now?' Rosanna's voice was weary. She longed for the privacy of her own room and wished suddenly that she could just leave them all, get on a plane and disappear. Even Carlo she didn't want to see now.

'I came to tell you that you must go—leave Sicily— as soon as the baby's born, whatever Carlo says. He won't drive you away. He feels sorry for you.'

Rosanna felt the poison drip into her system as Maria chose the words to inflict hurt and humiliation. Pity? Carlo felt pity? Dear heaven, was there no end to it? How much more would she have to bear? It had to stop.

She stood up. 'There's no need to say any more, Maria. Believe me, I want to go as much as you want me to. And now please excuse me.'

In her bedroom the maid was drawing the curtains. Christina took one look at Rosanna's stony face and sent the girl out. Clucking and chatting at random about nothing, her hands were gentle as she undressed Rosanna and put her between the warmed sheets.

'Thank you,' Rosanna dismissed her and was alone at last, the untouched lunch forgotten by both women.

Drained and numb, Rosanna felt no urge to weep. Tears might have been welcome. How could she now face her husband? And what did he want from her? Why had he brought her back to Palermo? Her mind went round and round in weary circles and nothing made sense. Even her husband had become a shadowy figure, a remote stranger whom she could hardly remember and had never really understood.

Rosanna got up to the fading light of late afternoon, showered and washed her hair. Sitting at the dressing table, she picked up a towel and began to rub her hair.

'Let me do that,' her husband said quietly.

Shock went through her. She hadn't heard him come in. Before she could speak, he had taken the towel from her hands and was rubbing her hair, gently and firmly, almost as though he enjoyed it. She closed her eyes, the feeling of his hands against her scalp bringing a deep pleasure that encompassed her whole body.

At last he finished. The towel dropped and their eyes met in the mirror. A quiver of feeling shuddered through her. In the half light he looked thinner than she had ever seen him. His skin was stretched tightly across the strong jawline and the wide forehead where deep lines were etched between the brows. More lines of weariness circled the blue eyes, half veiled, their expression unreadable as he regarded her intently.

Rosanna looked away from that penetrating gaze, suddenly conscious of the thin lawn of her robe that barely covered her. She raised her hands, pulling the edges together, with a feeling of panic at the thought that he would see her bulky figure.

'Are you ashamed of your body?' Carlo demanded harshly.

'No,' she blushed at his question.

'Then don't hide it from me.'

'Please, Carlo, what is it you want? I'm trying to get dressed.'

'I'm not stopping you,' he commented mockingly.

Rosanna sat, miserably conscious of her own conflicting emotions. Her throat tightened at the informal clothes he wore—broad shoulders emphasised by the clinging light sweater, and the long lean figure in tight narrow cords. She longed to touch him, to smooth the frown from his face, caress the strong throat and weave her fingers into his hair. Achingly she wanted to cling to him, beg him to hold her, kiss her.

Instead she stood up and moved away, pulling the robe tightly round her. Carlo stepped forward and bent to the lamp on her dressing table. A click and the darkened room was flooded with soft light. He straightened up and looked at her, from her damp hair across the softened bloom of her face, down her throat to the breasts outlined under the robe and on to the roundness of her body where she carried the child.

Suddenly she was no longer afraid or ashamed. She lifted her head proudly and looked back at him as his eyes returned to her face. Before either of them could speak, a tremor shook her as the baby inside gave an enormous kick. Her hands flew to her body and she bent forward slightly.

'What is it?' Carlo was at her side, his arms round her, and for a moment she leaned against him, enjoying his concern. Then she laughed lightly.

'It's nothing—just your son kicking. Sometimes it feels as though he's planning to kick for Palermo!'

His eyes widened with surprise, the blue eyes

flaring with sudden emotion. For a moment his face softened into a slight smile, then he moved away from her. 'My son?' he drawled.

'Oh, no, Carlo, don't start that again, please!' Her voice sounded anguished and she strove for calm. 'Just tell me why you've brought me here and then go.'

He didn't answer immediately, and she waited.

'There's been talk about our marriage,' he said harshly. 'Questions have been asked . . . where you are . . . why we're not together.'

Rosanna raised her head, curious to know where this was leading. As always when he had something difficult to tell her, Carlo turned his back.

'I wish you to remain in Palermo now till the baby's birth,' he finished baldly.

'I see . . . what has been said, Carlo?' she asked.

'No one dares to question my private life to my face,' he answered hotly, 'but someone wrote to my sister Luisa in Canada . . . and she's concerned about the stories she's heard, that our marriage isn't real, that the child isn't mine, can't be mine,' he went on painfully . . . 'that you were pregnant when you arrived in Sicily. . . .' He was speaking jerkily and she knew how unbearably difficult it was for him to tell her what she had to know.

'I wrote to Luisa reassuring her, but she's become . . . persistent. She wants to visit. I tried to persuade her to wait till the baby's born, but she's impatient. And now she's invited herself. My brother-in-law is coming with her and they're bringing their youngest child, Gabriella. She's my niece and also my goddaughter.'

'I see.' Rosanna was trying to take it all in. 'You'll enjoy seeing them.'

'I ... yes, but it won't be easy.' He moved and looked directly into her face, his eyes searching, seemingly demanding something of her. 'While she's here we'll have to behave as a normal couple. I tried to persuade her to stay with Maria, but she ... they ... don't get on too well. Luisa wants to stay here ... to get to know you.'

Now she understood. He didn't want her in Palermo, but his hand had been forced by his sister and by the gossip about their marriage. He would have to stop seeing Maria and behave like a husband. Well, she was not prepared to help him.

'So what do you want of me?' she asked coldly.

'For the time they're here, you and I will share this room,' he answered, 'and when we're with them we'll have to behave as though ... we had affection for each other ... as any other couple.' Wearily he threaded his fingers through his hair. 'I hope my brother-in-law won't be able to stay more than a few days, weeks at most.'

'*Weeks?*' Rosanna was horrified.

'I like it no more than you, Rosanna,' he said impatiently, 'I'll be in as little as possible, but I insist on your discretion.' He began to pace up and down. 'You'll probably see more of Luisa than I, and I expect you to support me as a normal wife would do.'

'You expect—you insist!' Rosanna was angry. 'And what if I refuse? What will you do, Carlo? Put me in my room on bread and water? Doesn't it occur to you to ask me? No, of course not. The great Carlo Vicenzi never asks—he just commands. Well, I won't do it. I'm not going to live a lie from morning to night—especially with a child in the house. I'm returning to Cefalu in the morning.'

'Whatever your feelings in the matter you'll do as I

say.' His voice was quiet and controlled, cold anger clear in his face. 'Of course I didn't ask. You would have refused, and we neither of us have a choice. What do you imagine I feel about it?' He breathed deeply, trying to control himself. 'I know what you think of me. You've made that only too clear, and I don't want this enforced intimacy any more than you. But Luisa's no fool. She'd know at once if I was sleeping in the dressing room. And then there'd be questions. Would you prefer that? Probings about our marriage—in the last weeks before the baby's born?'

Rosanna sat down heavily on the bed, her body shaken with the unaccustomed emotion. She clenched her hands, willing herself to ease up, relax. It was all too much. Seeing her husband again, aware of his anger and indifference, was more than she could handle. How could she face an intimate life with Carlo when she loved him and was in the last stages of her pregnancy, vulnerable, emotional? –

Restlessly she got up and moved to the window, unaware of his eyes following her, resting on the picture she made against the soft evening light that outlined her figure. He sat quite still, watching her as she leaned wearily against the window, prising comfort from the cool of the glass against her heated face.

'There are choices,' she said wistfully. 'You could let me go to England and have the baby there. Then you could come over to collect him and we wouldn't have to meet again.'

'No!' he thundered at her, all patience, all gentleness gone. 'My son is going to be born here, in Sicily—a Sicilian. Don't try me too far, Rosanna. If you hatch any wild schemes I shall have no pity. You've not felt my anger, but by God, you'd know it if you took my child away!'

His child. So he did believe her! Rosanna felt a sudden surge of intense joy and turned her face to him. But he was already at her side, gripping her shoulders with fierce hard fingers as he began to shake her. In fear and trembling she put her arms protectively round her body, shielding the child from his violence.

Carlo dropped her arms as if the touch of her burnt him, his face white, nostrils flared, eyes suddenly bleak. 'Please, Rosanna, just do as I say... or I won't be responsible for the consequences!'

She swayed, suddenly faint, and he caught her, lifting her and carrying her to the bed. As he laid her down her robe fell open and his eyes went to her body. She turned away from him, trying to cover herself, afraid of his disgust. The tension seemed to fill the room and she lay quite still, fearful of what he would do next. Then she felt his hands on her, gentle and warm against her skin, turning her towards him as he sat down beside her.

'Rosanna, you can't be afraid of me?' His voice sounded oddly strangled. 'You don't think I could ever hurt you?'

She kept her eyes closed, afraid to look at him and betray her feelings. 'No, Carlo,' she whispered, 'I know you wouldn't hurt the child.'

He didn't answer or move away, and Rosanna opened her eyes. He was bending over her, closer than she had realised, and his face had lost the shuttered look of moments earlier. His eyes, half closed, were intent on her mouth. Before she could move he bent his head to find her lips with his.

Desire flooded her at his touch and she tried desperately to control and conceal her longing, to remain cool and unresponsive under his lips. His kiss deepened. No longer gentle, he parted her lips with his and explored her mouth with savage hunger as if he couldn't stop. Her hands crept to his head, her fingers holding him close as she kissed him back, unable to hide the longing for him that swept her body, the aching need that only he could satisfy.

The kiss went on and on as she clung to him, eyes closed, aware of nothing but his mouth against hers, the scent of him in her nostrils.

And then he broke from her hold and straightened up. For a moment he stood looking down at her, eyes almost shut, his breathing uneven. Then he moved.

'It's best if you rest now,' he said tonelessly. The next moment the door closed behind him and she was alone.

CHAPTER NINE

THE arrivals lounge of the airport was crowded, and Rosanna was glad of Carlo's protective arm round her as they made their way to the barrier. The plane from Canada had landed and passengers were beginning to drift out from the Customs hall. She watched her husband as he towered over other men, his slim figure and handsome head a target for several female stares, drawn by the magnetic attraction of which he seemed totally unaware. Vanity was certainly not one of his faults, Rosanna mused, and he would be contemptuous of the admiration he roused in strange women if it was pointed out to him.

The day was warm and he was dressed in a tobacco-coloured light jacket and toning slacks, a cashmere sweater rolled at his throat. She had dressed carefully when told he wished her to come to the airport, and was pleased with the pale blue slightly starched cotton dress that flowed crisply from a small Peter Pan collar with full sleeves fastened at the wrists in wide cuffs. She wore comfortably high-heeled shoes that had been made for her and carried only a pouch bag embroidered to match the flowers on the hem of her dress. They made a handsome couple, outwardly the picture of relaxed happiness. But inwardly Rosanna was full of trepidation, dreading the next weeks and the pretence that Carlo was demanding of her.

'Uncle Carlo!' It was a shriek that rose above the hum of conversation as a tiny figure came rushing through the crowd to hurl herself at Carlo. 'It's me . . .

me ... me ...!' she shouted in English, the Canadian drawl loud and clear. 'Don't you recognise me, Uncle Carlo?'

Carlo laughed and lifted the small girl into a firm embrace, kissing her fondly. 'Hey, young woman,' he said in English, 'what have you done to yourself? You haven't grown up while my back was turned, have you?'

'Yes, I'm all growed up. Do you like me? Am I pretty?'

Rosanna looked with amazement at her husband's laughing face, and the affectionate embrace in which he held the child.

'Yes, you're pretty,' he told her, 'but you must let me say hello to your parents.'

He walked towards a couple advancing slowly in the wake of their daughter. Brother and sister kissed and the men shook hands.

'Now I want you to meet Rosanna.' Carlo turned to her with outstretched hand to draw her forward. 'Darling,' he said, pulling her to his side, 'this is Luisa ... and James who is long-suffering enough to stay married to her.' Rosanna smiled shyly as everyone laughed. 'And this is Gaby,' he went on, 'my niece and also my goddaughter.'

Gaby was the only one not smiling. Carlo still held her and her eyes were on a level with Rosanna's as she looked gravely into Rosanna's face, assessing what she saw.

'You're pretty,' she said at last, 'but not as pretty as Mummy.'

'Gaby!' her mother gasped. 'Please forgive her, Rosanna.' Disregarding Rosanna's outstretched hand, Luisa moved forward and embraced her warmly. 'At last!' she said, smiling. 'I'm so happy to be here.'

'I hope I may claim a brother's privilege.' James advanced and kissed her gently on the mouth.

Carlo put Gaby down and pulled Rosanna away. 'That's quite enough, thank you,' he said firmly. 'She's mine, you know, and other men don't have any rights to her favours.'

Rosanna blushed fiercely, furious with Carlo for his expert performance, almost as though he might actually be jealous.

'Come, let's go.' Carlo led the way out to the car where Enrico and the porter were stowing the luggage, while Carlo wrapped Rosanna into her fur jacket.

'I want to sit with Uncle Carlo,' Gaby demanded, and sat herself firmly on his lap. Nestling into his shoulder, she continued to stare at Rosanna as the car began to move out of the airport.

'She looks like Auntie Beth, Mummy,' she said next.

'Yes, darling,' her mother replied.

'Is she going to have a baby like Auntie Beth'?

'Yes, she is.' Luisa looked at Rosanna. 'When is it due?'

'Not long now.' Rosanna was still shy of them all.

'Will it be a girl or a boy?' Gaby asked next.

'Which would you like?' Rosanna asked, smiling.

'I think I'd like a sister,' she decided.

'This baby will be your cousin, not your sister, Gaby,' her mother corrected.

'Will the baby come home with us, Mummy?'

'Not to live,' Rosanna put in, 'but perhaps you can come and visit.'

'Will you bring the baby to see us?' Gaby asked seriously.

There was an awkward silence as Rosanna went fiery red. She didn't dare look at her husband and hoped he would answer.

'The baby will be too young to travel for a while,' Carlo said evenly, 'but you'll probably be able to come and see him here.'

'It's to be a boy, is it?' James asked.

Suddenly Gaby intervened. 'You're pretty when you smile,' she looked at Rosanna. 'Just as pretty as Mummy.'

'Thank you,' Rosanna said lightly, 'that's the nicest thing anyone has said to me in ages.'

She felt Carlo stiffen at her side and a hush fell in the car as Rosanna realised what she'd said. Luisa's eyes clouded slightly and James looked enquiringly at Carlo. It was the child who relieved the tension.

'I'm going to be sick,' she announced defiantly.

'No, you're not,' her mother said firmly, and reached to take her from Carlo. 'Come and sit with me.' Gaby snuggled down in her mother's lap and promptly closed her eyes.

Luisa spoke quietly. 'She's been spinning like a top all the way. Everyone on the plane spoilt her with sweets and chocolates. As soon as we get home I'll tuck her into bed and she'll probably sleep the clock round.'

Rosanna looked at the sleeping child, long black curls, dark eyelashes lying on softly tanned cheeks, the pretty wool suit crumpled, the white socks and patent shoes dusty. 'She does look tired,' she said softly.

At home everything was in readiness. Luisa and Christina greeted each other affectionately and took Gaby upstairs. The men settled to drinks and Rosanna turned to leave them.

'Where will you be, darling?' Carlo held her for a moment, and she felt breathless at his touch.

'I'll just make sure about lunch, I think, and leave you to yourselves,' she answered.

A quick kiss on the mouth and he released her. She turned away to hide her flush, but not soon enough.

'Still able to make her blush, Carlo? I congratulate you. You're a lucky man,' James grinned.

'Yes, aren't I?' Carlo drawled, and only Rosanna could hear the mockery in his voice.

Upstairs all was quiet, and Rosanna knocked on Luisa's door.

'Come in.' Luisa was changing.

'I'm sorry,' Rosanna said quickly, 'I'll come back later.'

'Don't be silly. Come in and talk to me.'

'I wondered if you'd like some tea or something to eat. Lunch will be at two if that's all right.'

'Great! By that time my stomach will have returned to its proper place. Tea would be lovely. Do you think we could have it up here away from the men?'

'Of course.' Rosanna wasn't happy at the thought of an intimate chat with her sister-in-law, but she knew it would have to be faced sooner or later. 'I'll ask Christina to bring it up.'

In the kitchen Christina looked rather penetratingly into Rosanna's pale face. '*Si, signora*, I'll bring it myself.'

'Thank you.' She turned away. 'I'm afraid there'll be extra work now, but you must ask for help if it's needed.'

'Thank you, but the Signor Conte has already arranged for more help. It is no trouble, but you know how considerate he is,' she said deliberately.

'Yes'. Rosanna moved to the door.

'*Signora*, the *signorina* Luisa ... she is ... I've known her since babyhood. She's a good woman with a kind heart. Here in Sicily when she was young, she didn't have an easy time. She has ... understanding . . . you can trust her.'

Rosanna was flustered. 'Of course, Christina, I know that.'

'You need a woman to talk to,' Christina went on bluntly. 'Me—I worry for you. First in Cefalu, alone all those months when a woman needs her man with her. And now here. . . . And all the time Signor Carlo, he is exhausted, back into himself as he was when Signor Luigi died.'

'Please!' The distress showed in Rosanna's face. 'I don't want to talk about it. We must both look after him as well as . . . we can.'

'Yes, but who's to look after you? You don't look like a woman happy to be with child. And it isn't good for the *bambino* to have a mother who worries and is lonely. This is bred into the baby.'

'No, Christina, please . . . no!' Rosanna's voice rose, 'I don't want to talk about it. We have guests,' she went on more quietly, 'and we must make sure they're comfortable while they're with us.' She looked entreatingly at the other woman. 'Please!' she stressed. 'I rely on you.'

The other woman's face softened. 'Very well, *signora*, I will do as you ask.'

'Thank you.' Rosanna relaxed.

She peeped into Gaby's room. The curtains were drawn and the child was asleep. Curled round her teddy bear, she lay against the pink bed linen. Carlo's niece. And she obviously adored her uncle. Those moments at the airport when they had greeted each other had given Rosanna a new insight into her husband. He would make a wonderful father. It was strange she had never thought about that. He would adore his child and show it. Achingly she wondered if the coming child would bring him happiness.

She heard Christina's step and closed the door quietly, making her way back to Luisa.

'Thank you, Christina, that's lovely, just the way I like it.' Luisa was sitting in a housecoat in front of the tea tray. Christina went away and Luisa sighed with pleasure. 'You know, Rosanna, I've been tempted to come before, but in the end I waited because I do love Sicily in the early spring. The hot summers that draw the tourists like flies do nothing for me. But the spring flowers, the soft, warm air, I love.' She stood up and stretched. 'Come and sit down. You must be tired. Carlo shouldn't have brought you to the airport—all those people, and nowhere to sit.'

'I wanted to come,' Rosanna said quietly, 'and I don't enjoy being treated as an invalid. Carlo knows that.'

They both sat down and Luisa poured. 'I understand you've been at the Cefalu villa,' Luisa commented. 'I rang several times and missed you.'

'That's right. I like it there, it's so peaceful and quiet.'

'So has Carlo been commuting?'

'No,' Rosanna hesitated. 'He came when he could,' she lied uneasily.

Luisa put down her cup with a clatter, and the two women looked at each other.

Rosanna guessed her sister-in-law to be about forty. Tall and gracefully built like Carlo, her hair was dark and curly, the eyes brown with long dark lashes. A straight nose, beautiful pale skin and a firm mouth and chin gave the face beauty and character.

'Rosanna,' Luisa asked seriously, 'do you love Carlo?'

Rosanna lifted her head and looked Luisa in the eyes. 'Very much,' she said firmly.

Luisa visibly expelled her breath. 'Thank God!' she said at last. 'So whatever the problem, it's not that.'

Rosanna looked away from those frank eyes, unable to add to what she had said.

'Can you tell me what's troubling Carlo?' Luisa asked next.

'No,' Rosanna replied baldly.

'Very well, I'll ask the question differently.' Luisa tried again. 'I know my brother well enough to know something's wrong. If you love him, and he obviously adores you and is proud of you, what is it?'

Rosanna sat without replying. She didn't dare tell Luisa the truth, that Carlo didn't love her, that he loved his sister-in-law, his brother's widow. That wasn't her secret to reveal.

'Do you know why Carlo is unhappy?' Luisa went on intently.

'I think so.'

'Then why can't you tell me?'

'It's up to him to tell you if he wants you to know,' Rosanna answered.

Luisa began to pace the room. 'I knew there was something. I sensed it on the phone. I thought if I came over I'd know at once what it was.' She stopped and looked at Rosanna. 'And I must tell you, Rosanna, I thought it was you, that you didn't love him, that you married him for his money . . . position.'

She sighed and continued pacing. 'I've hoped for so long he'd find someone who cared for him. Always the people he loved—mother, Dad, Luigi—they didn't . . . value him. Then when Luigi died he stopped caring . . . about anything. He withdrew even from me and I knew he blamed himself for the way . . . he died . . . in his place. It was a terrible time. Carlo became ruthless, indifferent, bored. Nothing mattered, nothing could touch him. There were women, of course. He's attractive and wealthy, and they've always run to him from the time he was a teenager. But they're not concerned about him—what he might want, need. . . . They're only interested in his wealth—and his virility. And he's not involved.'

She stopped again and looked down at Rosanna, her hands clasped in her lap, her eyes downcast. 'And then I heard about you,' she went on. 'And it didn't fit, unless he'd fallen in love with you—madly, the way I'd always hoped he would one day.'

Louisa sat down close to Rosanna and looked at her. 'So?' she asked. 'Why? What is it? Why can't you come and visit us with the baby?'

Rosanna didn't answer. 'For some reason there's no chance you'll ever come to Canada. Why, Rosanna? Why?' She put her hands to her cheeks. 'I wish I knew what it's all about.'

'I'm sorry I can't tell you' Rosanna said quietly. 'But I think you could help him by just accepting things as they are. I'm sure he'll tell you everything . . . when he can. But at the moment—well, maybe he just can't talk about it. Can you understand that?'

'Mm . . .' Luisa looked deeply into her eyes, probing, searching. Then she sighed. 'Very well,' she said calmly, 'I'll leave it.' A sudden smile lit her face. 'Perhaps I've gotten into the habit of fussing over Carlo, treating him still as though he's my little brother and needs my protection.' She leaned forward suddenly and kissed Rosanna's worried face gently. 'Let's forget it and just enjoy being together.'

That night at dinner Rosanna felt surprisingly relaxed and content. She had rested after lunch and then helped to bath Gaby, who had woken briefly, only to fall asleep again after a light supper. Luisa and Carlo were talking, James putting in the odd comment and Rosanna watched them.

James she guessed to be in his late forties, broad and muscular, rugged but not strictly handsome. Grey eyes set in a fair-skinned face, his hair was blond, soft and receding slightly. As powerful a personality in his way as her husband sitting opposite. Carlo's face with its ruthless set of mouth and chin was relaxed tonight, talking and responding, at ease in his own home with those he loved.

The bond with his sister was obvious in the lazy teasing she received from him, an undercurrent of affection in his voice. The two men had unmistakable respect for each other, and Rosanna thought how much more pleasant Carlo's life would be if the two people here tonight spent more time with him.

Luisa was wearing a low-cut dinner gown in deep blue velvet, cut low across the breasts, a beautiful sapphire necklace round her throat. Rosanna had dressed with care in one of Valli's creations and enjoyed the feel of the crisp organza that floated round her body and legs, the deep amber colour showing her creamy skin, the low neckline just hinting at the new fulness of her breasts.

She hadn't seen her husband alone. He must have showered while she slept and changed in the dressing room. When she came down he was dispensing drinks. At her shy 'good evening' to everyone, he had stopped talking, his eyes intent on her as he looked across the room. Whether he was pleased with her appearance or felt critical she didn't know. His 'hello, darling' was belated and cool, and she sat down away from him.

'How's business?' James was asking.

'Good, as usual,' Carlo responded casually.

'I wish you'd get out,' said Luisa, suddenly

passionate. 'I've always wanted you to leave it.'

'I might yet surprise you, dear sister, and do just that.' Carlo spoke lightly and it was difficult to tell if he was serious.

'I hoped you would after . . . Luigi . . . died,' she said quietly.

'That wasn't the moment, *cara*,' Carlo said evenly.

'Would you come to us, Carlo, when it's all settled?' James asked.

'No, I'm afraid not.' Carlo was adamant.

'Oh, I do wish you could come out to us,' Luisa's face flushed with pleasure at the thought. 'You'd love it, Rosanna. The climate is hard in a way—very hot in summer and very cold in winter, but it's ideal for children. So much space—mountains, lakes—every kind of sport to enjoy.'

'It does sound lovely,' Rosanna murmured quietly, not looking at Carlo.

'Well, brother, would you let her come out to us while you're sorting things out?'

'No,' Carlo said curtly, 'Rosanna wouldn't want to go alone.' He stopped, realising he'd spoken sharply and turned to her. 'You wouldn't want to go without me, would you, *carissima*?'

She looked back steadily, straight into his eyes. 'No, darling, of course not. I couldn't enjoy it without you.'

For a moment he looked stunned, bewilderment in his eyes. Then he laughed awkwardly and turned away, a flush rising under his tan.

Rosanna moved. 'Coffee?' she asked. 'Shall we move?'

In the next room she went to the turntable and selected a record, putting it on low. As they sat down the haunting strains of *Scheherazade* sounded through the room, and Rosanna leaned back, her eyes closed, listening to one of her favourite pieces of music. Dimly aware of voices and the clinking of cups, the smell of cigar smoke and the perfume of flowers from the balcony, she thought sadly that she would always remember this evening.

James sat down beside her. 'I think you and I should become acquainted, don't you?' He pulled an ashtray towards him. 'Let the two of them reminisce.' He looked across at his wife. 'You probably know there's a special bond between them. But now we have you in the family, perhaps the account can be squared. I can get a little of my own back.' He smiled down at her and she was aware of his charm. 'Tell me something about yourself,' he demanded.

Rosanna smiled, but didn't speak, her eyes on her husband as he bent to Luisa's face.

'Are you jealous?' James murmured.

'No,' she spoke unthinkingly, 'I'm just glad you're here and he's happy.'

There was an astonished silence from the man at her side. 'But isn't he generally happy? I always thought Carlo's problems were now behind him ... his mother, his brother's death, Giovanna. He always seems happy to me.'

'Yes, of course,' Rosanna evaded the issue. 'As you said, he's very fond of his sister.'

'Rosanna,' Carlo's voice cut across the room, 'dance with me.'

Rosanna sat stunned with surprise. 'I can't dance ... now,' she grinned, 'with my bulk!'

'Yes, you can.' He came across the room to her, holding out his hands. 'Come, we haven't danced for a long time,' he said softly. 'I'll show you how.'

As if mesmerised by the light in his eyes, the caress in his voice, she allowed him to pull her up. He took her in his arms and held her loosely against him, one hand down her back, the other under her hair, stroking the soft skin, moving his finger slowly across the nerve ends he knew so well.

'Kiss me,' he whispered, bending down to her face.

'No, Carlo!' She tried to pull away, but he held her firmly.

'I said, kiss me,' he insisted, and took her lips with his mouth, forcing her face up to his. It was a slow kiss in time to the music, his lips moving against hers, deeply, sensually, and she could feel his heart thudding against her. As always she responded, swamped by love and desire. His kiss hardened demandingly as he stood still, both hands at the back of her head as his lips moved to her closed eyelids, her temples, softly lightly touching, before he let her go.

The other two were dancing, and Rosanna looked straight into Luisa's eyes, full of delight and happiness. Carlo's sister thought she had witnessed their love for each other. That was why Carlo had asked her to dance, Rosanna realised suddenly as she sat down and he relinquished her hands. He had wanted to show his sister that there was nothing wrong with his marriage, that he could rouse his wife to passionate response. And he had succeeded. Luisa would ask no more awkward questions.

Oh, dear, Rosanna thought unhappily, Carlo was clever. And suddenly she hated him again as she had that morning when their honeymoon had ended so abruptly almost a year ago.

They were gone. Gaby had insisted they wave from the airport terrace until the plane was out of sight, and Now Rosanna felt tired and more than a little depressed. It had all gone beautifully, and she knew

Carlo was pleased. Walking with him to the waiting car, she sensed the renewed tension in him, the withdrawal. While his family were around he had been relaxed and carefree, but as soon as they were out of sight, he returned to his taciturn self, cold and indifferent.

Rosanna stared through the glass at Enrico's back. 'Do I go back to Cefalu now?' she asked indifferently.

'No,' Carlo replied coolly. 'Albini wants you here in Palermo to keep an eye on you. It shouldn't be long now.'

She didn't answer. There was no need. After the past three weeks he knew she would do whatever he wanted. She had been marvellous, and he didn't know, didn't guess how easy it had been. She had simply let down her guard and behaved as the loving wife she longed to be. After that first day Rosanna had been determined to make the most of her situation. When they were all together she had touched Carlo lightly, affectionately, as she would have done had they been in love. She had looked at him, her heart in her eyes, not troubling to hide her feelings—cheerful, amusing and strangely content.

Even at night she had coped. At first it had been agonising to have him so near, the intimacy of the shared bed bringing back memories she had pushed to the back of her mind. But after a few days she had lost her inhibitions, and one night when she had woken to find herself lying up against him, his arm round her, their bodies curved into each other, she had begun to pull away. But his arms tightened round her and she had thought how silly to try and escape when she was where she most wanted to be.

He never disturbed her, coming quietly into the room at night only when she turned out the light. He would slip into bed in the dark and lie rigidly on his side, until his even breathing told her he was asleep.

'I want to thank you,' he said suddenly, 'for ... everything. I know it hasn't been easy, the last weeks, but it all went off better than I could have hoped.'

Rosanna didn't answer. She didn't want his thanks for her performance. The last weeks had been more real to her than any life they had shared since their honeymoon. But she could hardly tell him that. 'I liked them,' she said quietly instead.

'And they love you,' he said evenly.

She looked at his profile and surprised an uncertainty in his averted face, almost as though there was something else he wanted to say.

But suddenly he leaned forward to rap on the glass partition. 'Here will do, Enrico, thank you'.

The car drew into the kerb and stopped. 'I have to leave you now,' Carlo said formally, 'I've an appointment. No doubt you'll be pleased to be relieved of my company from now on,' he added harshly.

He got out, snapped the door shut and bowed very slightly at her through the glass before he turned and walked away.

The telegram lay on the silver salver in the hall. Addressed to her, it was from England, and Rosanna had a sudden premonition of bad news.

Christina was fussing about resting and a drink, and Rosanna agreed she was tired, didn't want to be disturbed. Walking unsteadily into her bedroom, she sat down heavily on the bed.

With trembling fingers she opened the envelope. The message was short and simple.

'Deeply regret to inform you your mother died last night. Parting peaceful and painless. Condolences. Martin.'

It was dated three days earlier.

CHAPTER TEN

THE gate creaked as Rosanna walked through it into the graveyard beyond. At the end of the gravelled path stood the chapel, closed and silent, flanked by two spreading cedar trees that dwarfed the tiny building. The day was stormy with black clouds low in the sky, and the wind sighing through the long grass weaving round the gravestones. Rosanna shivered.

At the side of the heavy oak door the notice was pinned under glass. 'Mrs. S. Dunham 2.30'. There was only the one funeral that afternoon.

Using both hands, she pushed open the door and walked inside. Bare walls and small windows set high into the roof seemed to echo the bleak winter day outside. No gleaming gold or candlelight softened the stark white of the altar or the unadorned wooden chairs drawn up in rows to face the lectern. A single urn held a spray of green leaves.

As she walked up the short aisle, Rosanna's eyes were riveted to the plain wooden coffin in lonely isolation on its catafalque, thick brass handles gleaming faintly in the afternoon light.

A sudden trembling seized her and she sank down on one of the chairs, shivering uncontrollably. She had arrived in time. Her brain seemed to be repeating it over and over, and it was only now she realised how frightened she had been that she might be too late for the funeral, unable to bid her mother goodbye.

And now at last the nightmare was real. Her mother was truly dead. Never again would she see the beloved face, hear the voice scolding or feel the warmth and tenderness of her mother's embrace.

Dear God, she'd made such a mess of everything! Would her mother be alive today if she had not gone to Sicily? Had she died of loneliness as much as any actual illness? And alone, while her only child was hundreds of miles away. Rosanna recognised she had been an idiotic fool, playing with her mother's life and her own.

And where had it all led? It had brought nothing but unhappiness and to her mother it had brought death. Bitterly Rosanna blamed herself. She had failed her mother, and she had also failed herself. She could only hope she would not also fail her baby.

As her mother's death had taken away her future, so it had released her from her bondage to her grandfather. She no longer needed the money, didn't want it. And she was free of him. She could break the fiendish, inhuman contract he had forced on her, and she could take her revenge for the death of her parents.

She would deprive him of the heir he wanted so badly. After the funeral she would disappear, change her name and lose herself in the life of a big city. Once the child was born, it would be hers, and she would love it and raise it alone.

Resolutely she closed her mind to her husband, what he would think and feel. She had left him no note. There was nothing to say. On the dressing table behind her locked bedroom door lay her rings. Carlo would understand what that meant.

Suddenly her control cracked, the tension and effort of the last twenty-four hours catching up at last. The pain caught her unawares and she bent her head as the sobs racked her body.

An hour later she turned her back on the new grave with its covering of fresh earth and the flowers she had brought. Dimly she was aware of several other people. Two nurses had sat through the chaplain's address in the chapel, and an old lady had stood by the grave, throwing some spring flowers on to the coffin as it was lowered.

'Rosanna?'

She turned. The old lady stood on the path behind her, dressed in a long dark coat and flat shoes, wisps of grey hair escaping from under the battered felt hat. The face that peered at Rosanna uncertainly was wrinkled, pale and tired, watery eyes blinking nervously.

'Yes?' Rosanna acknowledged, and stopped.

'My name ... er ... is Hilda.' The woman was hesitating, as if unwilling to come any closer. 'I ... you don't know me,' she went on awkwardly, 'but I promised your mother ...'

Rosanna interrupted eagerly. 'You knew my mother?'

'Er ... yes, me and her, we were ... friendly. I work at the clinic and we ...'

'Please,' Rosanna took the old lady by the arm, 'won't you come and sit with me in the car? Out of the wind?'

'Er ... no, not really. I just wanted ...' Her gaze dropped to Rosanna's rounded body and her face lit up. 'Oh, you want to sit down? Of course, love,' she beamed, 'off we go!'

The chauffeur handed them both into the hired car and the old woman looked round nervously at the luxury of the interior.

'Please,' Rosanna begged, 'will you tell me ...?'

'Oh, yes.' The other woman pulled herself together.

'Your ma and me, we were friendly,' she confided. 'It all started 'cos we both had daughters, I mean. And your ma did love to talk about you. So proud of you, she was ... your looks, your wonderful job. Anyway, I've got a message.'

Rosanna held her breath, sudden emotion constricting her breathing as she watched the other woman open her capacious handbag and rummage inside.

'I know I've got it here somewhere,' she mumbled, '... there it is!' she said triumphantly, and pulled out a white handkerchief neatly folded. Slowly and carefully she opened it out, her large, roughened hands gently lifting a chain and locket that Rosanna recognised instantly. It was silver with a picture of her mother's mother inside it.

'Sylvia said to give you this,' Hilda said gravely, holding it out to Rosanna. 'When I go, Hilda, she said, you see her—mark, my Rosanna will come—and give her this. Tell her my wedding ring I'm taking with me, but this I want her to have. That's what she said.'

Rosanna was crying unashamedly as she took the locket and cradled it in her hand.

'And something else,' Hilda went on slowly, knitting her brow, concentrating hard to remember. 'Tell her not to fret. That's it.' Hilda smiled as she remembered. 'I know I'm going, she said, but I want to go. Ask her to forgive me and tell her one day she'll understand.' Hilda paused. 'Oh, yes,' she went on, 'and tell her I love her. Don't forget that, Hilda, she said. Oh, dear, we went over and over it together till I got it right.' She sighed with relief. 'I've been that worried, but my Daphne said I'd remember, that I'd get it all right. And I have, haven't I?' she ended, smiling happily.

'Thank you,' Rosanna was still crying, 'thank you so

very much. You don't know how much it means to me.'

'There now, love, you mustn't cry. It's not good for the baby and your ma wouldn't want you to cry.' The old lady wrinkled her brow, puzzled. 'Funny, Sylvia never said nothing about your being married and expecting . . . oh, well, it probably slipped her mind.'

She gathered her things together. 'Now I must go, dear. It's been nice meeting you and I've enjoyed our little chat, but I have to get home. My Daphne will be expecting her tea.'

The plane dipped and circled as it descended to land, glimpses of sea and rocks flashing past the small window as Rosanna felt the baby move sharply inside her.

Dusk was closing in as she stepped down on to the tarmac, an anxious stewardess at her side. Slowly she walked into the Customs hall where a chair was found for her while she waited for the taxi she had ordered.

At last her body was protesting at the punishment it had suffered in the past two days. She felt drained and longed only for bed.

The previous afternoon while the hired car travelled swiftly towards London, she had looked out at the green of the wet countryside thinking over everything Hilda had told her.

The message from her mother was more poignant than it was intended. One day she would understand, her mother had said. What would she understand? That her mother didn't want to go on living without the husband she adored . . .?

She, too, wondered what her own future life would hold without her husband. Would the baby compensate for the man she loved? And what about the baby deprived of his father? What would she tell him as he grew to manhood?

Ten miles outside London she had leaned forward and quietly direct the chauffeur to Heathrow Airport.

And now she was too weary to think or worry if she would regret returning to Sicily. She could only guess how much more heartache and hurt still lay ahead. All she knew for certain was that she couldn't deprive Carlo of his child or the baby of its father. For herself she felt only emptiness and knew that her childhood was finally over, buried with her mother in an English grave.

A few moments later she was making her way through the usual waiting crowd, walking blindly and wearily to the exit where her car was waiting.

For a minute she didn't see the man who straightened at her approach and stepped towards her.

'Rosanna!'

Bemused, she looked up into her husband's face and came to a faltering stop. She hardly recognised him. His hair was rumpled, his unshaven face showed a dark stubble of beard, and there were deep shadows round his eyes which were red-rimmed. The immaculate suit was crumpled as he stood, silent, and still looking at her.

'You've come back,' he said jerkily.

'Carlo!' she stammered. 'How did you know . . .'

'I've been waiting' he said huskily.

She looked at him, unable to focus her mind, trying to understand what he was saying, what he was doing at the airport when he didn't know she had gone. . . . Her eyes began to swim and she trembled with weakness, swaying on her feet.

Carlo caught her to him convulsively, his lips against her hair, his breathing ragged against her face.

'*Madonna mia!*' he whispered.

'Carlo,' she began again faintly, 'I . . .'

He bent to pick her up. Holding her close, he strode with her to the exit. Before they reached the car she was asleep.

The baby was born in the early hours of the following morning. When the pains began Rosanna was dimly aware of cheerful nurses and lights swaying above her on the ceiling as she was wheeled through the hospital corridors.

Then Dr Albini was bending over her in a green gown, smiling broadly. 'Well, Rosanna, this is it. Let's get to it.'

She smiled sleepily, thinking it was all very well for him to be so cheerful.

After that she was conscious of little. She remembered calling for her husband. And he was there. As she clung to him, he held her firmly, talking to her quietly, reassuring.

'I'm here, *bella*, just hold tight. You're doing fine . . . just fine. . . .' Once she heard his quiet chuckle 'You've a stronger grip than I knew, *carissima*. I shall be the one with bruises tomorrow!' And she giggled weakly.

And then at last it was all over, and someone put her son into her arms, a small bundle with a fuzz of black hair. And she laughed with sudden bursting happiness.

'I knew it,' she whispered against the soft silk of his cheek, 'you have your father's eyes.'

And then she slept.

During the next days Rosanna craved only sleep. They woke her to eat, to drink and to feed the baby, but she saw no one and was refused all visitors. It was the fourth day that she opened her eyes to sunlight and flowers which filled her room.

The baby's cot was by her bed and he was asleep. As she looked down at him, one tiny fist against his cheek above the blanket, her planned resistance to him melted and the beginnings of motherhood tugged at her heart.

In the days that followed she lived only for him, thinking of nothing beyond the quiet room, the soft coming and going of nurses, and closeness with her son.

It wasn't only that he looked so like Carlo. But, holding him close, talking to him softly, she watched his dawning awareness of the world around him. Arms and legs not yet under control would dart out in all directions. And his head would jerk at unexpected noises. Happily fed, he would fall asleep in her arms and she would hold him, till cramp finally forced her to put him back into his cot.

He was just a week old when Carlo walked into the room. She was feeding, holding him close, wondering if he had finished.

Carlo stood inside the door watching them both, his eyes intent, his expression unreadable. Rosanna blushed.

Quietly he came across the carpet to her bed. 'You're better.' It was a statement, not a question, and his voice was gentle, oddly tender.

'Yes.' She flushed as his eyes dropped to the baby at her breast.

'Here, let me take him. He's falling asleep.'

He shed his coat and bent down to her. Softly he touched her breast, pulling the nipple gently out of the tiny mouth, and Rosanna quivered at the feel of his warm hand against her skin, the colour rising from her throat. He lifted their son expertly and without any awkwardness, holding him firmly, rubbing his back to bring up his wind.

The baby looked tiny between his hands, the small head with its soft fuzz of dark hair against the brown throat locked with longing. Where had he been the past week? Had those hands been caressing Maria?

She felt tears prick behind her eyes and clamped down on her thoughts, controlling emotions that could only lead to storms and more heartache. She looked up to see Carlo walking up and down with the baby, talking to him, odd whispered, meaningless endearments, and sudden pain shattered through her. The two beings she most loved were together, the man's feelings evident in the way he held his son, the baby's love and dependence only just beginning.

'I think he needs expert help.' Carlo's voice intruded into her thoughts.

She smiled and pushed the bell by her bed. The young nurse who appeared looked with amazement at the tall elegant man holding the baby.

'Would you take him, Gina, please? I think he needs changing before he falls asleep.'

'*Si, signora.*' She took the baby, her face tinged with colour as Carlo smiled down at her. Nervously she smiled at Rosanna and left them.

Carlo walked away from her to the window. 'Albini tells me he wants to keep you here for some weeks to build up your strength.'

'Yes.'

'I'm afraid I can't keep the family away much longer—they've been agitating to come. But I'll try to stop them bothering you. They can see him in the nursery.' He turned. 'I suppose you'd prefer that?'

'Whatever seems best, Carlo,' she said dully, realising why he had come.

'There is something else, Rosanna,' he began almost hesitantly. 'Your grandfather wants to see you.'

She didn't say anything, but lay back, pulling the sheet up to her chin as she returned his look coolly, her eyes guarded.

'I told him I'd ask you,' he went on.

'What does he want?' Rosanna spoke carefully.

'He wants to see you before you leave.'

She winced and hoped he hadn't noticed. 'I'm afraid that isn't possible,' she said coldly.

'I believe . . . there's something special he needs to tell you.'

'He didn't choose to be available to me last year when I needed him. Why should I see him now he wants something from me he can't buy?'

Carlo looked across at her steadily. 'Perhaps because you have your whole life in front of you, and his is ending.'

'I'll think about it, Carlo,' she said finally, suddenly tired of fencing with him.

Surprisingly he came to sit beside her on the bed. Picking up her hand, his fingers gently stroked her palm. 'Rosanna,' he asked softly, 'would you consider staying on in Sicily?' His voice was low, persuasive.

She looked at him in amazement. His eyes were hidden as usual, but the jaw was clenched and she felt the tension in him. Somehow she sensed the answer was important. Maria had warned her this would happen. Why did he want her to stay? Had Maria changed her mind, decided she didn't want to bring up the baby after all? Why couldn't he be honest with her, tell her what he wanted from her and why?

Suddenly nervous, she snatched her hand away. 'I

don't understand what you're asking, Carlo. I have . . .
plans of my own . . . in England.'

He got up abruptly and turned his back to her. 'It
doesn't really matter what I mean, does, it, Rosanna?'
he demanded harshly. 'There's still someone waiting
for you, more important than your child . . . someone
who'll have you back even though you've been
married and borne another man's baby . . . and
abandoned it.' His voice rose with anger and his face
as he looked at her was pale with emotion.

Was it possible . . . could he be jealous? This talk of
a man . . . Rosanna's hand stole to her throat and her
face softened.

'Perhaps it's better this way, for all of us,' he went
on tautly, 'even for the child. Why should his life be
blighted by the knowledge that his mother abandoned
him as a baby?'

'No, Carlo, please don't,' she begged. 'Please don't
say any more . . . I can't answer you now. I don't
know what to say.'

He moved to stand at the bottom of her bed, looking
down at her, his face tightly closed. 'Very well,' he
said woodenly, 'you're right—there's no point to any
more talk. I'll make all the necessary arrangements for
your departure . . . and your move to England.'

'I don't want anything from you, Carlo,' Rosanna
whispered.

'You're still my responsibility. As the mother of my
son you will continue to be so until you marry again.'

He turned away and walked to the door.

'Carlo . . .' she pleaded, 'don't let's part in anger. I
don't . . . I didn't mean to offend you . . . please, I . . .'

'Offend me?' he interrupted, his voice icy. 'Whatever
makes you think you could do so? His mouth curled
with scorn. 'After all, this is precisely what was

planned from the beginning. We've merely arrived at the end of the contract.'

Everything looked exactly the same, and each detail of her last visit remained crystal clear in her memory as she followed Sophia up the thickly carpeted stairs of the Villa Orsini. Briefly Rosanna wondered again what her grandfather could possibly want from her.

After their last stormy meeting at the hospital Carlo hadn't come again. When finally the doctors agreed that she could go home, she had sat, her farewells said to the nursing staff, the baby in her arms, waiting for her husband. But it was Enrico who had driven them home, where Christina had welcomed them, and Rosanna had taken the baby to the sunlit new nursery wing and Angelina, the young, shy nanny Carlo had engaged.

On her dressing table she had found the small package with her name on it. Inside, the card in her husband's bold handwriting had stared at her. 'To the mother of my beautiful son, in gratitude.' And on the back: 'Roberto for his great-grandfather who made his birth possible, Luigi in memory of his father's brother and Harold because his grandmother would have wished it.'

Lifting out the exquisite earrings, Rosanna had held them against her face, the black onyx hanging like heavy pearls, surrounded by a myriad tiny diamonds. Cradling them in her hands, she had cried, the tears melting much of the bitterness of the months that lay behind.

As before, Sophia stopped before the heavy wooden door and the same secretary ushered her through the outer room into a different one beyond.

'Signora Vicenzi,' he announced, and left.

Roberto Orsini was in bed. The same watchful

nurse in starched white was hovering as Rosanna stood by the door and waited. He tried weakly to heave himself up against the banks of pillows, and the nurse moved to make him comfortable before she heeded his dismissal. 'Please,' she said quietly as she passed Rosanna, 'no excitement.'

As soon as they were alone Rosanna wished she hadn't come. The awkwardness was there between them, and with it came the memory of their last meeting and the things that had been said.

He was ill, Carlo had said, and this was obvious to Rosanna, watching his efforts to fight for breath. Was he dying? She was here only because she knew her mother would have wished it.

'Come here, child, where I can see you.' His voice was markedly weaker than she remembered.

Rosanna hesitated.

'Come . . . I can't see you there.'

She moved to sit on the chair drawn up by the bed.

'Thank you for coming . . . there are some things I want to say to you before I. . . .' He breathed heavily in the silent room, his eyes closed, forcing the energy he sought to rise through his throat muscles. Rosanna waited, her eyes going round the dark, high-ceilinged room, dominated by the huge fourposter bed, its heavy hangings casting the room into shadow. She felt a sudden stirring of compassion at the suffering she was watching. Strangely, her grandfather seemed a lonely old man, ill, dying perhaps, with no family at his bedside, and the image she had carried for so long of the cruel tyrant faded from her imagination.

'Your mother,' he said weakly, 'I want to talk of your mother.'

She stiffened.

'Did you ever write to tell her you were pregnant?'

Rosanna gasped audibly. He had known all the time that her mother was still alive!

'Yes,' he answered her unspoken question, 'I knew. Her illness, the clinic, your reason for coming . . . all of it.' His eyes opened wide suddenly and looked straight into hers. 'You'll think me cruel to keep you ignorant. Perhaps it was. But I wanted . . . needed that child. Had I given you the money there would be no Roberto today.' His head fell back, worn out by the effort he had made.

'Your mother,' he went on, 'I was afraid for her. your father was a warm, loving man, but not a man of substance, either in wealth or character. I wanted a marriage for her where she would be sheltered, protected . . . her health. It was never good. She wasn't strong. Even as a child she had breakdowns . . . nervous illnesses. I wanted her to have her children in security and comfort without any threat to that—very precious health. . . .'

Rosanna waited while his laboured breathing died and he was able to continue. 'I underestimated her.' He smiled gently. 'She loved your father tenaciously, with a strength I never knew she had. And so she left me. For many numberless, lonely years I regretted . . . many things, especially the ultimatum . . . but my pride stopped me from telling her so.' His face twisted with emotion, and Rosanna found the tears rise behind her lashes. 'I always hoped she would return,' he whispered hoarsely, 'but she didn't, and perhaps that's been my punishment.'

When he stopped his heavy breathing was the only sound in the room. Unable to keep still, Rosanna got up and walked to the window, staring at the closed shutters, her back to the old man in the bed behind her.

'Did you ... did Carlo ... does Carlo know the real reason I came to have the child?' she asked quietly.

'No.' She turned to face him as he twisted his head, trying to look at her. The effort was too much, and instinctively she moved back to the bed, sitting down again at his side.

'Carlo would only agree to the contract if the marriage was temporary. He didn't want any involvement, and was worried that you were young and might become fond of him and ... refuse to leave.' He cleared his throat. 'So I told him you had someone in England ... a man you loved and wanted to marry, who would wait for you. ...' his voice tailed off. 'That was the only way I could get Carlo to agree.'

Rosanna sat rigid, her face white, her eyes dark with pain. So the web of lies and deceit was complete. Carlo had believed all along that she was in love with another man. Did he believe it still? she wondered. It explained many things ... his contempt of her, abandoning her at Cefalu ... so many puzzling things fell into place. She gripped her hands together tightly, forcing control over her body, fighting the weakness that threatened her.

'My dear ...' the weak voice of her grandfather reached her in a hushed whisper, 'have I damaged you irretrievably? That's why I wanted to see you. To thank you for the boy, and to know if you're all right.' He coughed painfully. 'I wondered—perhaps—did you—have you come to love your husband? Have I to add your unhappiness to my other sins?'

Rosanna straightened up and looked down at the old man as his hand groped for hers on the blanket. She bent and took it lightly in her own cold one.

'No, of course not,' she said firmly. 'But the time has come for me to leave Sicily and begin my new life.'

CHAPTER ELEVEN

THE candles flickered back at Rosanna from the darkened windows of the crowded restaurant overlooking the ancient pier of Mondello Lido. The cream of Palermo society was enjoying the exquisite food, luxurious surroundings and discreet service of one of Sicily's foremost eating places.

Glittering chandeliers, their lights reflected in huge gilt mirrors, shone down on to sparkling jewels and the shining faces of beautiful women who had spent most of the day preparing for the evening.

Rosanna sat alone with Carlo on the curved plush velvet sofa of their alcove, the clink of glasses and low hum of conversation drifting by, isolating them from other diners.

'Coffee, *signora*, *signore*?' Carlo ordered, and Rosanna looked at her husband.

Returning from the Villa Orsini earlier in the day, she had found an excited Christina waiting for her.

'*Il Signor Conte, signora!*' she had whispered.

'Here?' Rosanna's pulse had fluttered.

'No.' Christina shook her head. 'On the telephone. He wishes you to dine with him tonight and will call for you at eight o'clock.'

Rosanna had hesitated over her dress. Black taffeta. She had never worn black before and wondered if for once Valli had made a mistake. With its long sleeves, plunging neckline and the way the material clung over her breasts and into her waist, it seemed more revealing than she cared to wear. But once dressed, the skirt falling in deep crisp folds to the tip of her high-heeled black sandals, she saw the stark simplicity gave her a maturity and glamour that was new.

And she put on the earrings. As they drifted in and out of her hair, the diamonds glinting, she knew she loved them as nothing else she had ever owned.

'May I smoke?'

Carlo looked across at her and she nodded, watching the flame light his face, showing the firm moulding of lips, the strong, clefted chin and the dark column of his throat. He was sitting at ease, long legs stretched out, and Rosanna's throat was suddenly dry with longing.

She put down her glass, fingers trembling, eyes down, fighting to keep emotion at bay, determined to enjoy the evening as doubtless the last she would spend with him.

Everything had been impeccably planned. A bottle of Veuve Clicquot on ice had been waiting at their table to which the smiling headwaiter had bowed them as Carlo greeted him by name. Cool, sweet melon with thin slivers of parma ham had been followed by freshly grilled sardines and a fruit sorbet to clear the palate before the Tournedos Rossini, the small fillet steaks in their creamy wine sauce. They had both refused a sweet, but Carlo had peeled a juicy peach and cut it up for Rosanna to eat.

And he had made every effort to entertain her, chatting pleasantly as though they had just met, telling her amusing stories of his travels all over the world, until the tension that had gripped her at the beginning of the evening dissolved in her enjoyment of the food, the superb wine and the beguiling charm of her husband's attention.

'Rosanna,' his voice intruded into her thoughts. He turned to her and his eyes narrowed, noting her downcast face, and the nervous play of fingers with the stem of her glass. 'Have you thought any more about staying on in Sicily?'

Her fingers tightened round the stem of the glass, but she didn't speak.

'Well?'

'But . . .' she stumbled, 'what about Maria?'

'Maria?' he echoed in astonishment. 'Did you think I'd let her bring up Roberto?' he frowned for a moment in concentration. 'No . . . she doesn't like children. And in any case, she's leaving Sicily.'

'Leaving Sicily?' Rosanna's voice was incredulous.

'Yes. Her father and I have finally found her a husband. She's wanted for some time to marry again, but it hadn't been easy. She's no longer young and she didn't have a dowry. But now there is someone—an aspiring politician, younger than she, and I've . . . given her a dowry which I felt my family owed her. So Maria will make him an excellent hostess and in Rome she'll live the life she enjoys.'

Rosanna sat stunned. After all the planning and waiting Maria had become impatient and decided to marry someone else! And once again Carlo was being rejected in his affections. And this was why he wanted her to remain in Sicily. He had no one now to supervise Roberto's upbringing. So she was to be used. And because the contract had ended he could no longer command her to do as he wished. Instead he had to persuade her . . . the dinner, champagne, charm. . . .'

'Well?' he was waiting for her answer.

She lifted her head and looked across at him, cool, assessing. Could she do it? Could she remain in Sicily, watching him with other women, bringing up their son, seeing him only when he came to visit the baby?

Before she could reply he leaned across the table, picking up her hand, unclenching it from the stem of her glass and looking down at her rings, a frown between his brows.

'Tell me,' he asked without looking up, 'why did you come back?'

She moved to pull her hand away, but his fingers tightened over hers. 'I . . . should have explained,' she began hesitantly, 'why I went, but it's been. . . .'

'I didn't ask why you went,' he interrupted her nervous babbling, 'I know that.'

She lifted her face at that. 'You know?'

'Certainly,' he said grimly.

'How?'

'Because I followed you.'

'No,' Rosanna's voice was low and angry, 'no one followed me. I was on the last flight to England that night.

His grip on her hand tightened painfully. 'I came home that night to find the bedroom locked,' he began, his voice strained. 'I thought you might be ill, so when I could get no reply, I broke in. When I saw you'd gone, I thought . . .' he cleared his throat, 'you'd been taken. I spent the next hours trying to find out who . . . where you might be. But there was no trace . . . no one knew anything . . . there was just a blank wall . . . nothing.'

'You mean you thought I'd been kidnapped?' she asked, incredulous.

'Kidnapped, possibly killed,' he answered harshly. 'I . . . I wasn't thinking too clearly.' His fingers clamped round her hand, and Rosanna bit back a strangled cry of pain as her rings cut into the soft skin of her palm.

'Eventually I went back into the bedroom,' he said jerkily, 'and I found your rings.' He realised suddenly how tightly he was holding her hand and relaxed his grip, his thumb rubbing gently across her palm. 'Then I knew you'd gone, of your own free will. I remembered what you'd said about going to England to have the baby.' He looked up from her hand into her face. 'Before midnight I was on my way.'

'But. . . .'

'I flew myself, used my own plane,' he answered roughly. 'Before morning I was with Mr Williams.'

'Mr Williams?' echoed Rosanna.

'Your solicitor. At first he refused to tell me anything. You were his client, and all information was confidential.' His jaw clenched. 'I wasn't polite.' He went on grimly. 'When I'd finished painting him a picture of you stranded, alone, without money . . . possibly in labour, he panicked and told me everything . . . your father, your mother's illness. And then I knew what was in that telegram Christina reported, that we couldn't find. And I knew also where you would be.'

He let go of her hand and sat back, his fingers on the stem of his glass, his eyes on the amber liquid.

Rosanna sat mesmerised, unable to speak or move, her eyes riveted to his face.

'Early next morning I came home.' He picked up his glass and drank the brandy in one gulp, throwing back his head, swallowing deeply.

'But, Carlo, wh-wh-wh . . .' she swallowed hard to free her speech. 'Why didn't you come after me? I might have . . . I mean, what if I'd . . . disappeared with the baby . . .?' her voice trailed off miserably as she remembered.

'Did you, Rosanna?' he asked huskily. 'Did you plan to leave me, take the child and disappear?' He leaned forward again and took both her hands in his. 'So . . . tell me, *cara*, why did you come back? You could have kept the child.'

Rosanna sat silent, her whole body quivering at his touch, the melting caress in his voice, some strange intensity of feeling that she couldn't name. She looked up into his eyes, but they were narrowed, unreadable in the drawn tension of his face. He was demanding something he wanted, some commitment, but he was giving nothing in return, promising nothing. . . .

Suddenly anger leaped into her throat and she recoiled from him, pulling her hands from his grasp. 'No, Carlo, no . . . .' He was playing with her again, gauging her emotions expertly to get what he wanted. 'Stop it!' she protested vehemently, her voice low and shaking with resentment. 'I won't let you manipulate me again. It was bad enough when you had the power to force me to do what you wanted, but this . . . persuading, cajoling . . . it's horrible, cruel!' She was close to tears. 'Why can't you leave me alone?' she demanded passionately. 'Let me go in peace without putting me through all this?'

She backed away from him in sudden revulsion and rose to her feet. Heedless of staring waiters, she ran past the astonished faces of other diners. Blindly intent only to get away from him, she rushed through the foyer and out into the night.

Uncertain in the dark, she turned towards the sea, stumbling towards the pier, tears streaming down her face, her hair blowing into her eyes, a slim dark figure running recklessly towards the water ahead.

Dimly she heard Carlo behind her, calling, 'No, Rosanna . . . no . . . dear God. . .!'

She panicked at the sound of his voice closing in on her, the dress and her high heels hampering her headlong flight.

And then he caught her from behind and his arms closed round her, dragging her back from the edge and the black water below, his breath hard and rasping on her face. He turned her in his arms and she felt the clamped steel of his embrace before his mouth closed over hers and she was engulfed in the savage fury of his kiss.

Frantically she fought to free herself, but he only tightened his hold and the kiss grew more violent, his hands gripping her arms so fiercely that a scream rose in her throat. The tears fell against her lips, but still he didn't relax his grip. Then her frenzy died and she clung to him, desperate for air, limp in his arms.

And at last he lifted his head and looked down into her face, the moonlight revealing the blazing fury in his eyes.

'Why is it,' he muttered, 'you have this power to madden me to violence?'

Without waiting for an answer he picked her up and strode with her back along the pier. Ignoring the lights of the restaurant, he made for the car and dumped her unceremoniously into the passenger seat, picking up a fur rug from the back and throwing it over her.

'Now cry,' he commanded grimly as he slipped behind the wheel and the powerful car roared out into the darkness.

Rosanna sat cold and mutinous. How dared he treat her as though she was an errant schoolgirl? She was a grown woman, the mother of his child, and he had no right to patronise her. She turned to tell him so.

'Save it, Rosanna,' he said mildly, his eyes on the

road ahead. 'Even you can't fight me while I'm driving.'

She relapsed into silence, suddenly weary. It was her first evening out since Roberto's birth, and she wasn't as strong as she'd felt earlier in the day.

On the motorway the sleek powerful car ate up the miles and neither spoke. Rosanna watched the Palermo sign flash past them as Carlo ignored it and drove straight on. Were they going to Cefalu? she wondered dully. She hoped not. She never wanted to see the villa again.

Gradually her trembling subsided and the warmth from the rug and the car heater penetrated her cold body.

'Wake up, Rosanna, we're here!'

Carlo spoke coldly and got out of the car, leaving her to make her own way in his wake. She could see nothing in the darkness, the only sound his footsteps crunching on gravel. Then a light sprang on ahead, and she got out of the car walking slowly, unwillingly, towards it. Inside she crossed the entrance hall towards an open door. Carlo was in the room beyond, putting a light to the logs in a large brick fireplace and Rosanna stood uncertainly in the doorway.

'I don't know what you're planning, but I'm not in the mood for social calls,' she said coldly. 'I want to return to Palermo.'

'Come in and sit down, Rosanna, the evening's not ended yet.'

'It's over for me, Carlo, and I've no intention of sitting down. If you won't drive me, please call me a car.'

'There's nowhere to run, Rosanna.' he sat down on one of the deep sofas facing the fire, and went on calmly, 'We're on the east coast of the island, just south of Taormina. All round us are deep woods, a stream from the mountains, and the house is hidden from the road some two miles away ... as also from the air, private in its own extensive grounds.'

Rosanna looked round the room with curiosity. It was wide and long, oak beams holding up a whitewashed ceiling. Built on two levels, one end was carpeted with three huge chintz-covered sofas facing the fireplace. On the upper level polished wooden floors with white rugs held a round Victorian pedestal table, while books covered one wall and full length glazed chintz curtains covered a second. Lights from low brass table lamps gave the room a cosy, welcoming glow.

'Very well, Carlo.' She came towards him slowly, weariness in her voice. 'Just tell me what it is you want from me now and then let me go. If it's about staying in Sicily, I have decided to go back to England at once—in the next days.'

He moved fast and was at her side, his face grim, his hands on her arms. 'You'll go when I'm ready to let you,' he said tautly, 'and first of all you'll answer my questions. Did your lover refuse to accept your child, Rosanna? Is that why you came back?'

She put her head back and looked up into his face, her own cool, unemotional. 'Please let go of me, Carlo,' she said coolly.

He walked away from her to lean against the surround of the fireplace, one foot on the fender, his head averted. She sat down abruptly, a sudden weakness in her legs.

'Well?' he demanded harshly.

What could she say? How could she tell him that her grandfather had lied to him about her reasons for coming to Sicily—having his child?

'Does it matter now, Carlo?' she asked quietly. 'You

have Roberto. That's what it was all about. Why rake over the past?'

'I have Roberto?' He turned to her in surprise. 'Your grandfather has Roberto.'

'I don't understand.'

'Having Roberto was your grandfather's condition.'

'Condition?' she echoed.

'What is this, Rosanna? You know why I agreed to . . . have the child, the reasons I wanted . . . needed the contract your grandfather offered? He told you last year when you came, didn't he?'

She shook her head.

'You mean you don't know?'

'I thought I knew . . . but not from my grandfather. I . . . understood you wanted the child . . . that was the reason.'

'A child by a woman I'd never met? Thank you!' His mouth curled sardonically. 'No wonder you have such a high opinion of me!'

Rosanna watched him, confused. How many more lies were to be uncovered? she wondered.

Carlo lifted a hand impatiently and raked it through his hair. 'I have to go back . . . a little,' he began, and sighed with some kind of frustration. 'After my brother was killed, I determined to rid myself of the family business, somehow, to find a life away from bodyguards and violence. In spite of heavy opposition from Giovanna's father and my own, I refused to take revenge for their deaths, to meet killing with more killing. They both tried to oppose me, but by then control of the business had passed to me and my word was law.'

He sat down away from her, his eyes intent on the fire where the dry logs were beginning to hiss and spit. 'It's not easy to relinquish the power and responsibilities of a business such as ours. I had to provide for the many families dependent on me for their livelihood, their security, and I had to find people I could trust to take over from me. It took years, and when your grandfather first approached me it was still not complete. But by that time I'd begun to think of my own future. Money was no problem. I had more than enough for the rest of my life. But I wanted to stay in Sicily, and I wanted something—needed something to do . . . work. I couldn't face spending my days in idleness.'

He paused, his mind on the past, almost as though he was talking to himself, thinking aloud, and Rosanna wondered if he had ever talked to anyone about it before.

'Your grandfather offered me his hotel empire on the east coast of the island. He had no son and he was ill . . . old. I would have a free hand, to run it as I wished, expand as I thought best, for the business and for the local inhabitants along the coast—ensure it wasn't spoilt.' His voice quickened with eagerness and she watched his eyes, for once unguarded as he turned round to her, the face alight with enthusiasm, much younger in the flickering light from the fire.

'A clever man, you're grandfather.' Carlo's face twisted wryly. 'With one stroke of the pen I'd have a new life . . . work and a purpose. I'd be able to stay in Sicily, leaving the west with its unhapy memories . . . restrictions.' He stopped, his face pensive. 'There was one condition. I had to beget an heir to unite my family with the Orsinis. By his granddaughter I would have a child to inherit after my death. The mother would return to England, and I would regain my freedom.'

'He leaned back in his chair, looking up at the

ceiling. 'Clever, did I say? Brilliant,' he mused ruefully. 'He knew exactly how desperately tempting was the plan he'd devised.'

Suddenly restless, he got up and moved away, pacing slowly across the room and back. 'After Giovanna died I had decided never to marry again. I wanted no more ... emotion, or commitment to another person. I had learned to mistrust all feelings—in myself and in others. The divorce would be valid for the mother, returning to England, but I would not be free to marry again ... in Sicily. And that was how I wanted it ... planned it.'

Suddenly he stood still, his head bent, his hands tightly clenched in his pockets. 'And then you arrived and it all began to go wrong,' he said quietly. 'We'd envisaged a young woman, hard, greedy for money, knowing precisely what she was doing, someone who would leave no mark on our lives. Instead you had ... spirit ... passion and innocence.' His voice sank to a whisper.

Then he straightened and walked over to the window, drawing back the curtains to look out into the blackness of the night.

'I knew I wanted you that first day before I had any idea who you were.' His voice was low and harsh. 'By the end of our honeymoon, I was in a spin, confused, more than a little frightened ... for myself, my own peace of mind. Your passionate response to me, your quiet undemanding companionship, your....' he smiled a little and turned his head to look at her across the room, '... obstinate independence ... they were all new to me. I had never met a woman like you.'

He went on painfully, 'I guessed you thought you'd fallen in love with me, but I was certain it was only the love a young girl would feel for the first man to rouse her to passion. And I knew it would pass.'

Rosanna looked away from him, her eyes wet, her feelings in turmoil.

'When we returned to Palermo, I withdrew from you, hoping my desire for you would pass, that—others could take your place.' He swallowed as Rosanna flushed. 'But it didn't work. Then I thought if we continued as lovers, I would become bored, satiated, as I had with other women in the past.'

He paused and Rosanna breathed in painfully as memory returned of those awful days.

'I was wrong,' Carlo said dully. 'The more we made love, the more I wanted you. I couldn't understand it. I didn't know myself. The only certainty was that I had to have you, that only you could bring me the joy and fulfilment I'd never dreamed existed.'

Wanting, not loving, Rosanna thought, trembling with emotion, responding to the deep intimacy of what he was telling her.

'By the time I did understand my own feelings, you had withdrawn from me,' he went on jerkily. 'Oh, you were still responsive, passionate. But you held back—eluded me, and I was sure I'd lost you.' He sighed, his shoulders hunched forward. 'I had never known jealousy, but with you I became obsessive. I couldn't bear to watch you with other men. That day I saw you with Manzini I went mad. I left Maria sitting there and chased after you like a love-crazed schoolboy, ready to strangle you if he was your lover. And all the time I knew of course you were only waiting for the moment when you would return to the man you loved,' he finished flatly.

He turned his head suddenly and smiled at her across the room, a singularly sweet smile. 'Pathetic, isn't it?' his mouth curved ironically. 'And just a little ridiculous.' His voice hardened. 'I'm almost old enough to be your father. You were only just emerging from innocence. Even if I could persuade you to stay for the sake of the baby, how long would it be before you tired of me, wanting to return to your lover?'

At last Rosanna spoke. 'Carlo, please. . . .'

He interrupted harshly. 'This man who loves you,' his voice grated with repressed emotion, 'what does he mean to you, Rosanna? Is it your love for him that keeps us apart?'

'No, Carlo,' she said quietly, 'there is no man who loves me.'

He spun round to face her.

'But your grandfather. . . .' Carlo's eyes were blazing at her, the intense blue almost black with emotion.

'I know,' she said gently, 'he told me today. You were afraid I . . . might fall in love with you . . . refuse you the divorce, want to stay on in Sicily.' She raised her head to him. 'So he invented a man I loved who was waiting for me.'

Carlo stood speechless as they stared at each other. She felt suddenly afraid, trembling. Had she misunderstood him? Did this change his feelings? Did he really want her, love her? He hadn't said so. Uncertain she stood up, her eyes wide with apprehension waiting for him to speak, to move. He didn't, and she turned away, suddenly sick with tension.

'Rosanna,' his voice reached her, soft and low. 'will you marry me?'

She spun round at last, her eyes wet with tears. 'Carlo,' she whispered throatily, 'we are married . . . don't you remember?' and her voice broke on a sob that turned into a tiny laugh at the look in his eyes.

'I know,' he said softly, 'but I want us to be married

... again, just the two of us, alone, making our vows to each other. Will you, *carissima*, love me and marry me?'

'Oh, yes,' she whispered through her tears, 'yes, please!'

At that he did move, coming to her side, pulling her down to sit with him, taking her ungently into his arms, his mouth urgent against hers.

'Tell me,' he demanded fiercely, 'I want to hear you say it.'

'I love you, Carlo,' she murmured shyly, 'so very much.'

'And I love you, my wife, with my whole heart and mind and body. Will you accept that from me and let me give you this house which was built for you?'

Tremulously she nodded. 'And will you come and live with me—in it,' she teased, 'or do I have to live alone?'

'Who else?' Carlo demanded arrogantly. Then his face changed. 'But why, *cara*, if there was no one else you loved, could I not reach you ... after our honeymoon?'

'I—thought you loved Maria, were planning to marry her.'

'Maria?' he was astounded. 'Who told you that?'

'She did,' Rosanna explained. 'And the reason for your marriage with me—the contract—was that she couldn't give you a child.'

He pulled her back into his arms. 'And you believed her?' he asked her lips against her face. 'But, how sick! I had no idea. She was always ... odd. Luigi hated her, you know, and I felt sorry for her because he wasn't a good husband. I tried to talk to him about it, but he said I didn't understand, that Maria wasn't normal. After he died, I felt responsible for her—but only as a brother.' He looked down into her eyes. 'You do believe me, Rosanna *mia*?'

She nodded. 'It's not important now.'

'You can't think I could love her, so cold and full of trouble when I had a woman in my bed, slender, desirable, warm, with a mouth that trembles against mine. . . .'

'I believe you,' she said, flushing slightly. Reaching up, she put her arms round his neck. 'But, Carlo . . . why, in Palermo you kept me imprisoned in the house. Didn't you trust me?'

His face became taut and he looked away into the fire. 'I couldn't make you understand, with your ideas about independence. I had still many enemies only too happy to know how much you meant to me, how they could hurt me through you.' His mouth curled sardonically. 'So I made certain I was seen with other women,' he said contemptuously, 'frequently. But even then I was terrified. All those months, working on this side of the island, I lived in fear something would happen to you. Enrico began to think me deranged. Each night I would travel like a maniac across the island—by car, by plane, by helicopter—I didn't care as long as I could spend at least part of each night in your arms.'

'And Cefalu?' Rosanna asked painfully, remembering the months of loneliness.

Putting one finger under her chin, he looked down deeply into her eyes, seeing the hurt. 'It was you, *carina*, who didn't want me. I came that evening, rushing like a madman from the airport, wanting only to be with you, to take you back to Palermo. But you wished to stay, to rest . . . and I was too proud to beg you to come back with me.'

'Oh, Carlo, that wasn't what I meant. . . .' she began, but he stopped her.

'Those months were terrible. I never want to go through anything like that again. No more separations, no misunderstandings.' He pulled her back into his arms. 'Kiss me,' he demanded, 'as you haven't done for endless months that passed slowly like years . . . alone, without you.'

Rosanna lifted her hands to his head, holding him gently, touching her mouth to his, tracing the shape of his lips with her own, the roughness of his chin against her skin. Her kiss deepened with love and longing and she opened his lips with hers, her body flaming with desire for his touch.

Then he groaned sharply and lifted her off his lap, turning her into his arms to lie on the sofa beneath him, kissing her fiercely, demandingly, as passion rose between them and her soft body moulded to his.

'Oh, Rosanna, Rosanna, I'm frightened to be so happy,' he whispered against her face. 'You won't ever leave me, will you?'

They clung together in the silent room, their hold on each other hard and painful, almost desperate, their hands and bodies reaching for each other, eagerly touching, finding familiar responses drowning in sensations long denied, as repressed emotions rose to the surface and time was forgotten.

It was Rosanna who surfaced first, saturated with happiness, dreamily content.

'Well,' she demanded lightly, tracing the outline of her husband's face with one finger, 'isn't it about time I was shown this house I've just been given?'

Carlo groaned heavily. 'Nagging me already?' he teased.

'But of course.' She smiled down at him.

'Now you've told me how rich you are, I shall be demanding morning, noon and night. There'll be no end to all the things I want!'

'As long as you want me,' he teased mockingly, 'I'll have to cope with it somehow.' He lifted her to her feet and saluted smartly. '*Ecco*, Signora Vicenzi, I will now take you on a guided tour of the house—for which, by the way, you haven't yet thanked me.'

Suddenly he bent down and picked her up in his arms. 'On second thoughts,' he announced arrogantly, 'tonight we'll confine our inspection to the master bedroom, and you can show me your gratitude in a manner befitting a new wife!'

Coming next month in Harlequin Presents!

727 LEADING MAN Claire Harrison
It's thrilling to have her first play performed on Broadway. But the lead actor's interpretation of her work is unnerving. He brings to life her innermost fears...and her secret desires!

728 RESPONSE Penny Jordan
A powerful Greek involves his temporary secretary in a whirlwind courtship—to avenge his sister's honor. Then when he discovers his mistake, he marries her—out of a sense of duty.

729 DESPERATE DESIRE Flora Kidd
When desperate desire takes hold of two strangers, they struggle against it. He, a half-blind man, is disillusioned by life. And she, because of a selfish man, is disillusioned by love.

730 FIDELITY Patricia Lake
Her hopes in ruins, a young woman hardly expects to meet up with the man of her dreams at a Swiss ski resort. Perhaps that's why their sudden marriage turns into such a nightmare.

731 SCANDALOUS Charlotte Lamb
A London photographer tries to sneak some pictures of a reclusive financier. Instead, she gets caught...caught falling for a man too rich and powerful to return the love of such an ordinary woman.

732 THE DARLING JADE Peggy Nicholson
Her careless driving causes a zany writer to break his wrist. But that's no excuse for him to frighten her, blackmail her and make her fall in love with him—all for his own amusement.

733 DARK AWAKENING Sally Wentworth
When a father objects to his daughter's whirlwind romance, the daughter rebels. And within the week, she is living in the Canary Islands home of a stranger—her husband.

734 BRIDE'S LACE Violet Winspear
She has every reason to hate him. But a young woman's plea to a wealthy Greek to keep her brother out of serious trouble will fall on deaf ears unless she agrees to marry him.

BARBARA DELINSKY
Fingerprints

Carly Quinn is a
woman with a past.
Born Robyn Hart, she
was forced to don a new
identity when her intensive
investigation of an arson-ring
resulted in a photographer's death
and threats against her life.

Ryan Cornell's entrance into her life
was a gradual one. The handsome
lawyer's interest was piqued, and then
captivated, by the mysterious Carly—a
woman of soaring passions and a
secret past.

RIDE A PAINTED PONY

by BEVERLY SOMMERS
The third
HARLEQUIN AMERICAN ROMANCE
PREMIER EDITION

A prestigious New York City publishing company decides to launch a new historical romance line, led by a woman who must first define what love means.

Available in October or send your name, address and zip or postal code, along with a check or money order for $3.70 (includes 75¢ for postage and handling) payable to Harlequin Reader Service to:

Harlequin Reader Service

In the U.S.	**In Canada**
Box 52040	5170 Yonge Street
Phoenix, AZ	P.O. Box 2800, Postal Station A,
85072-2040	Willowdale, Ontario M2N 5T5